Jackson has completed his Service and now is travelling the world aimlessly. He knows what kind of man he wants, but can never find him. When Octavian appears to him one morning, Jackson is unsure of what to do with the naked dream-man in front of him. Octavian only briefly hesitates before disappearing again. He is a recluse, and Jackson is determined to fuck with him before moving on in his travels. It is not that simple for Octavian . . .

Covert Master
Copyright © 2022 Crawford Rhine
ISBN: 978-1-4874-3671-1
Cover art by Martine Jardin

Published by eXtasy Books Inc

Look for us online at:
www.eXtasybooks.com

COVERT MASTER
ROMANIAN CHRONICLES 6

BY

CRAWFORD RHINE

CHAPTER ONE

An excerpt from the diary of Jackson Jurgovan.

June 10, 2019
Luzurne, Switzerland
This morning I am headed to Zurich by train.
Hungover from my last night in Luzurne.
Party by the lake last night turned into a total orgy.
There were four marked men there, which was a nice change.
Went back to the hotel with a huge Swiss man named Gunther. I think he was a forester of some type, but I couldn't really understand him.

Gunther was taller than me and I loved how he towered over me while he bent me in half and fucked down into me. Too bad he had a skinny dick, but it was long enough to give me pause. We fucked three times before I told him to get out.

Caught the train to Zurich at eleven and should be there by one. After eating lunch, my hotel room should be ready for me to check in.

I had drunk way too much at the party and after sleeping it off on the train, I realized that I was super-lucky to have gone back to the hotel with Gunther who was a real gentleman. Marked men weren't supposed to display such risky behavior, but I had been incredibly lucky so far in my life and I continued to press my luck. My father would have been quite disappointed in me, but I was sowing my oats, and they were wild.

I was living in a world full of men, the huge majority of them non-marked. Non-marked men, or NOMARs, were sexually attracted to women, which our world did not contain. Marked men, like me, were sexually attracted to men and therefore were highly prized in this world. We were called marked, because on the very moment of our thirteenth birthdays, each one of us received a blue mark on the side of our face—each one as unique and different as a fingerprint. Mine was a brilliant blue flame that ran from the bottom of my earlobe to the middle of my chin. I was quite proud of it.

I woke up on the morning of my thirteenth birthday, to see my mark. I had slept through whatever miracle happened. Although the mark hadn't appeared until that morning, I had felt it coming for quite a while. I had already begun to feel sexual urges about the older boys in my school, so I was not surprised to see the blue mark staring at me from the mirror.

I remember asking my father if there had been other marked men in our family. He told me that he didn't know anything about our family, since my grandfather had died so early in his life. There were no pictures or family history left to him. Dad had seemed okay with the appearance of my mark, but also looked worried for me.

It was a dangerous world for a marked man—full of traps everywhere. I learned a lot that first year as many older boys and even men tried to seduce, bully, or fast-talk their way into my pants. I was bigger than most kids, so I was lucky to escape most of these interactions unscathed.

I found myself attracted to older men most of all. I'm not sure if it was their experience or their fully formed masculinity that did it for me, but I was all about them. I finally lost my virginity to one of my father's poker buddies a couple of years after my mark appeared. Once I had a taste of sex, it was all over for me and that was all I could think about.

I went to The Service Academy when I turned sixteen and

it was there where I learned how to properly service a man, sexually. The SA was a school only for marked men, and I reveled in being around so many guys like myself. There were no other marked men in my town that I knew of.

When I turned eighteen, I entered The Service. This was a program for marked men where an agency would match up a marked man with a very wealthy NOMAR for a period of a year. The NOMAR basically got a sex slave for a year, and the marked man got a million dollars for each year he stayed with him. I couldn't wait to be rich and I dreamed of a sexy NOMAR daddy whom I would fall in love with.

My time in The Service didn't quite work out for me the way I wanted it to, but I had no regrets. My Master, Sully, was an overweight Italian mob boss. I was not really attracted to him at the start, but eventually found his clumsy advances charming. He really liked me and the mob had beautiful Italian men in it, so I was always happy to ride someone else's cock.

Sully and his crew taught me how to protect myself—how to use a blade and how to fire a gun. They also taught me how to hide money from the government, which I didn't think I would need to do, but it was nice to know. Sully kept me in the Service for four years, so I had a huge payday at the end of my Service. I would always be grateful for the protection that the mob provided for me, and that was probably why I traveled through Europe without a bodyguard with me.

Switzerland was a very safe country, but I would definitely have to contract with a protection company before I went any further into Europe. Some NOMARs would love to kidnap me and tie me onto their beds. The laws were very strict about that, of course, but NOMARs could be crazy when they were horny.

The Zurich Hauptbahnhof was the largest train station I had ever seen. It was very busy, with loads of people standing on the platforms and many more moving from one place to another. There were multiple restaurants, stores, and even two luxury hotels inside the station. I took my time looking around, but also keenly aware of who was watching me or coming too close to me.

Making my way to one of the taxi stands, I made eye contact with a driver in a black Mercedes sedan. I rolled my suitcase up to the trunk and said, "Storchen Zurich, please."

"American?" the driver asked, looking surprised.

"Yes," I answered with a friendly smile.

"Very nice," he said as he put my suitcase into the trunk and rushed back to the driver's seat. I slid into the back.

Once the car was in gear and we had pulled out into traffic, I added, "Although, like most Americans, I believe my family is from here in Europe somewhere."

"Probably east of here," the driver said immediately, like he had already been thinking about it.

"Why do you say that?"

"Your look reminds me of someone from Bulgaria or Romania," he answered without taking his eyes off the road.

I caught my reflection in the back window. I had dark hair that was slightly curly, even though I kept it shaved close to my head except on top. My complexion was darker than most, but that was because I tanned so easily, or so I had always told myself. My dark eyes were accentuated with a streak of shiny gold that made them sparkle most of the time. Most people took that sparkle as humor or mischief.

"Huh. I never thought about that before. I assumed it was Italy maybe. My father doesn't know much about our family history."

"Definitely not Italy," the driver told me. "My hobby is guessing people's nationality as I pick them up in my cab, and I have seen many people who have parts of your look and they almost always are from that area."

"I believe you," I said with a chuckle as I looked out of the window at Zurich. The business district reminded me of New York City a little bit, but the part of the city near the river had classic Old-World charm.

My hotel was everything I wanted it to be—unique, located downtown, and high class. My room was spacious and the king-sized bed made me itch for action. Too bad that I was hungover when I arrived. All I wanted to do at that point was get something to eat and retire early.

Fate had other plans for me. The hotel recommended an awesome restaurant down the street. I was soon seated at a table in a very cute banquette. I was too distracted by looking at pictures on my cell phone to notice when the waiter arrived.

"Good evening," the waiter said to me.

I looked up from my phone and almost dropped it. The waiter was smirking down at me, and he was absolutely gorgeous. He had brown hair with streaks of blond, and a matching beard to go with it. He was mocking me with his dark eyes, and his mouth had lips that were turned down at the ends into a frown, although I thought there was no way he was sad. I loved how neat and tidy his beard was and the European styling of his hair.

"Hello," I finally said. I saw his dark eyes flick to the electric blue mark on the side of my face.

"I'm JP."

"Jackson," I said with a smile. "What does JP stand for?"

"Jean Paul," he said as he shifted from one foot to the next. He seemed nervous now that he knew I was marked. "May I get you a cocktail or a glass of wine, Jackson?"

"I would love a *cock*tail, JP. What do you recommend?"

He blushed above his beard. "I recommend the Absinthe Martini."

"Ah, the green fairy. Okay, I'll take one of those."

JP was tall and thick. I was immediately turned on by him and imagined what his muscular chest would look like if he wasn't wearing that turtleneck sweater.

"Very good, sir." He turned to walk away and I noticed what a nice ass he had.

"Well, there goes my plan for the night," I said into the air as I put my phone down on the table and picked up the menu.

JP was back and had composed himself. "One *cock*tail," he said as he put my drink down on the table.

"I hope that's not the only one I will be getting tonight."

"Mine's quite a bit larger and, of course, not green."

"JP!" I said firmly.

The waiter blushed furiously.

I let him out of his discomfort. "That's okay, JP. I like bigger."

"Would you like to order now?"

"I thought I had already ordered you for the night, JP."

Now he was really flustered. I seductively sipped my martini.

"Do you want something to eat, sir?"

"I'm definitely eating something, JP."

He looked over his shoulder at the station where the waiters were clustered. There was no one around. JP leaned into me and said, "Listen. I'll fuck you from here to Basil, but you gotta let me get my job done or I'll be fired."

I made an impressed face. I loved a man who took charge. "Okay. What time does your shift end?"

"Eleven, sir."

"Perfect. I'll take the barley soup and the vegetable curry."

"Very good." JP turned and left me.

I had more of my drink and maintained a very professional demeanor for the rest of the meal, which was delicious. I had another drink before being ready to leave.

JP brought me the check and I paid it, leaving him a big tip.

I also handed him my card.

"Come to the hotel after you leave work." I had written the name of my hotel on the card.

"What room number are you in?" he asked as he stared at the card.

"Have the desk attendant call me from the lobby and I'll let you know." I had learned a long time ago not to give NOMARs too much information or leeway with me or they would have taken advantage. I had to be safe since I had no protection here.

"Okay. See you then."

"And JP?"

"Yes, sir?"

I stood up so that we were eye to eye. "I'm counting on you following through with your promise. You better fuck me all night long."

I watched as his Adam's apple bobbed up and down his tanned throat. "I will do as you command, sir."

"Will I have to command you?"

He laughed and flashed a brilliant set of teeth. "You probably could just lie there and I would still be in heaven."

I pressed my body against his as I brushed past him, leaned in, and said, "Well, I'm not going to just lie there, so you're going to need to bring it."

CHAPTER TWO

An excerpt from the diary of Jackson Jurgovan.

June 10, 2019
Zurich, Switzerland
Arrived in Zurich at mid-day. The city center is like any other big city, but cleaner and less scary. My hangover has finally gone away and I am feeling more like myself — hungry and horny!

Staying at the Storchen Zurich hotel. It is fabulous and very safe. I love Switzerland because the people treat you like you are fabulously wealthy, even if you aren't.

There is a very cute outdoor coffee shop right across from the hotel that I can't wait to try. Nothing says Europe to me like sitting out on the sidewalk and drinking coffee. I love that they have plants and flowers strewn all about like you are sitting in a garden. I can see the coffee shop from one of the windows in my room.

Went to a great restaurant named Alpina Pescatore, where I met a very handsome waiter named JP.

I have invited JP back to my hotel and I am waiting for him now.

I made sure that the hotel employees at the front desk knew that I was going to get a visitor by eleven thirty. I told them that I did not want them to send him up immediately, but to call me first. I tipped them heavily to make sure my wishes were followed.

Since I had more than two hours to wait for JP, I decided to take a nap so that I would feel more like myself by the time he arrived. I set the alarm, stripped, and crawled under the covers.

I slept like a log. Waking up feeling completely refreshed, I jumped into the shower and spent the next half hour manscaping my body to perfection. I loved the thought of JP being just as tall as I, and I couldn't wait for him to arrive so that I could get my rocks off.

My body was ringing like a bell by the time the hotel phone rang.

"Hello?"

"Mr. Jurgovan, this is Amir at the front desk."

"Yes?"

"You have a visitor waiting in the lobby."

"Is he alone, Amir?"

"Yes, sir."

"And how does he appear?"

"He seems nervous, sir."

"That's good."

"Did you check his ID, Amir?"

"I did, sir. I gave it a long hard stare."

"Excellent. You can tell him my room number now, Amir. Thank you."

"You are most welcome, Mr. Jurgovan. Your guest will be up shortly."

You can say that again, Amir.

"Thank you, Amir." I hung up the phone and undressed. I wanted there to be nothing to stop JP from ravishing me as soon as I opened the door. I knew it was way too desperate, but I had an itch that needed scratching and I didn't want to wait.

The knock on the door came sooner than I expected. I walked to the door and looked out the peep hole. It was JP, and he was alone. I pushed the latch down, but only opened the door far enough to clear the frame. Walking back to the bedroom, I hoped that the waiter was getting a good view of my ass.

"Wow," JP said breathlessly as he backed into the door, closing it.

"Like what you see, JP?"

He came into the bedroom and looked around. "You are very wealthy?"

"I am comfortable."

"You have a lot of men then?"

"Not because I am wealthy. Do you want a drink?"

"I'll take beer, if you have it."

"I have it." I walked over to the fully stocked bar in my suite and pulled a German wheat beer out of the fridge. I popped the cork on it and handed it to him. "You are very handsome."

"Danke," he said with the practice of a man who had heard this compliment many times.

"Have you never fucked a marked man before?"

"No, but I have been propositioned by several of them before."

That news shocked me. "You were asked to fuck them and you turned them down?"

He took a sip of the beer and said, "They were old and wrinkled. Not like you."

"I like that you have standards." I held up my glass of Coke and said, "Cheers to fucking your first marked man."

He walked over to me and clinked his beer bottle to my glass.

I placed my glass on the bar, dropped to my knees on the heavy carpet and began to unzip and unbutton JP's black pants. I could feel the heat pouring off of his crotch and his masculine scent hit me like a slap in the face as soon as I had his zipper open.

"Let's see what appetizer the waiter has brought for me," I said as I unhooked his pants and they feel to the carpet. His boxer shorts were close behind.

"Mm, Swiss sausage. My favorite!" I told him as I looked up while encircling his big cock with my fist. It was hot to the touch and already halfway filled with blood.

Leaning forward, I slowly swallowed his big prick and heard him gasp in delight above me. His cock tasted sweaty and gamey, like he had worked all day. Fortunately, I didn't mind that at all. I ran my tongue all over the velvety soft cock head and hardening shaft as I moved it back and forth between my lips.

My ability to give blowjobs had improved over the years, but it was always secondary to my skill at fucking. I tried my best with JP and saw him rise to his hardest state under my ministrations. He was so big that I had to lick up and down the outside of his shaft in order to get him all wet.

JP was handsome as all hell, but he was passively letting me blow him while he drank his beer. I knew that he was not the man for me at that very moment. I needed a man who took charge away from me, even though I loved to be in charge— even craved it. In order for me to truly experience extasy, I had to be dominated by a man who knew what he was doing.

So far in life, I had not found that man, at least not in JP. It wouldn't stop me from letting JP fuck my brains out, but it made me a little disappointed at the same time. Hopefully my dream man would find me soon, but until then, the handsome Swiss waiter would do nicely.

I looked up to him with my mouth full of his cock, because I knew this usually drove NOMARs insane, and I saw that it had the intended effect on JP as well. He put his beer down on the end table with his mouth slightly open. He reached down and lifted my chin even further back so that he could really look into my face.

"This is amazing," he almost whispered.

I pulled his big wet schlong out of my mouth and said, "If you think this is amazing, you are in for a real treat."

He leaned down and pulled me to my feet. "I am ready to fuck you now."

Direct . . .I like that.

I lifted the hem of his shirt with one hand and pulled it over his head. I was delighted to see that his brown hair was all over his chest in curly little tufts. With the other hand, I pushed him on the chest until he fell backwards onto the sofa.

Having previously imagined this scenario, I had prepared for it by putting a bottle of lube on the floor at the base of the couch. I grabbed the bottle now, squirted the silky gel into my hand, and began to massage it onto his cock.

JP moaned, closed his eyes, and threw his head back onto the top of the sofa.

That just confirmed my suspicions that most men would have settled for a hand job over a blowjob or even a fuck sometimes. There was something about a hand on your cock that just felt like nothing else.

Once JP's cock was hard and wet, I climbed onto the couch facing him and lowered myself to my knees. I had to elevate to reach the top of his long cock with my ass, but once I did, I could feel the heat of his cockhead on my puckered hole.

"You ready for this, virgin boy?"

He laughed and said, "I can't wait. I feel like I might explode."

"Not yet," I said with a snicker. I blew out a big breath, willing myself to relax.

I pushed my hips down and felt JP's cockhead push through my anal ring. My hole stretched to accommodate his big piece of meat. The mixture of pain and pleasure that I derived from the stretching was unbelievable. I pushed again and felt my asshole expand as the waiter's fat shaft pushed inside me.

"Fuck, that's nice," I said huskily.

"So hot and so tight."

I looked down at JP and said, "Well, don't sound so

surprised."

"No, I didn't mean—"

"I'm just joking with you."

I made one final push and slid all the way down onto his lap. His hot cock was fully inside me and I savored the feel of it. I considered myself a pretty talented and intellectual person, but there was nothing in the world that I liked better than to be mounted on a fat tool.

Opening my eyes, I looked at JP, who was sporting a huge fucking grin.

"That good?" I asked.

"The best thing that has ever happened to me," he answered without losing his huge grin.

"Jesus. The pressure is on me now to deliver."

"You could just sit there just like that and it would still be heaven."

"Well, I'm certainly not going to just sit here. Time for the show." I started to bounce on his cock, my head back and my eyes closed. I loved the way my anal ring stretched around his hard shaft as I rode him.

We both came within seconds of each other—JP shot his load deep in my guts and I shot mine all over his hairy chest. I was breathing heavily when I put my head on his shoulder and said, "That was something."

JP laughed and said, "Sure was."

"Shall we go again?"

"Ready when you are."

"That's impressive."

"Now, I have the pressure to deliver on me."

I stood on the sofa, popped his cock out of my ass, and said, "And you better deliver. I need you to go at least two more times like that before I can get a good night's sleep."

"Sleep is over-rated."

I grabbed his hand and pulled him off of the sofa. We

walked to the bed, where I lay down on my back and pulled my legs up and back onto my chest. "Big words, big man."

The handsome waiter raised one eyebrow and climbed between my legs. He fed his big cock back into my eager hole.

"Big cock also," I muttered as I arched my back and my eyes rolled back into my head.

CHAPTER THREE

A n excerpt from the journal of Jackson Jurgovan.

June 11, 2019
Zurich, Switzerland
The waiter, JP, turned out to be a great find. He was able to fuck and recover within minutes in order to be able to do it again. It's a beautiful thing when you find a man who can reload so quickly.

As soon as he leaves today, I want to shower and go get coffee at the shop across the street that I like so much.

I don't have any plans for today except to rest this afternoon and maybe doing a little sight-seeing tonight.

I plan to schedule a boat tour of the city later this afternoon.

I either need to do laundry in the next few days or go shopping and buy some new clothes. I'm not opposed to buying new, but the prices here are really steep, even for someone with money.

I saw a very cute chocolate fondue set in one of the store windows walking to dinner last night. I will probably purchase that for Dad for Christmas. He loves chocolate, and the Swiss make the best.

When I woke up early in the morning, my ass was burning from the fucking that I had received from JP. He was sleeping beside me, snoring softly. He looked lovely on the expensive linen sheets of the hotel, but he had to go.

One fatal flaw of mine to finding someone was that no matter how infatuated I was with them, once they fucked me, I was done with them and ready to move onto the next man. That was why I thought that I would never find the one man who would be able to overcome this flaw in my personality.

When I had been called to Service, I knew that this issue was going to come to a head, and it did. First, the man who had called for me was not my type at all, so there was never any attraction on my part. Secondly, I was ready to trade him in the second day of my Service.

But I didn't. Sully was a very nice Master. He taught me everything he knew about running a business, making money, and keeping the money that I made. I would be forever grateful to him for that knowledge, and of course, for the four million dollars that he gave me at the end of my four years with him.

The sex was not great, but I learned to satisfy him in a way that we both could enjoy. Sully didn't mind having a good orgy every once in a while, so I was exposed to a variety of his friends and peers. I also kept myself busy in his absence by fucking almost anything that moved. That kept things fresh and interesting for the two of us, which was key.

"You up already?"

I looked down at JP and said, "It's hard to sleep with your ass on fire."

He looked chagrined. "Sorry about that."

"Don't ever apologize for giving me the fucking I was asking for."

He suddenly grinned and asked, "Want to go again?" He pulled back the covers to reveal his full-grown morning wood.

"Who am I to turn down a sausage for breakfast?"

I leaned forward and wrapped my lips around his big cock. His skin was hot and smelled musky. I gave him a tug with my hand and pulled him towards the shower. I would finish up with this man in the shower and kill two birds with one stone, so to speak.

Later, after I was clean and JP had left a happy man, I made my way to the coffee shop across the street. The espresso was just as good as I had hoped it would be and the croissants were even better. I took a seat outside facing the sidewalk so that I could do a little people watching while I enjoyed my coffee. It was a sunny day with just a little chill to the breeze that occasionally blew through the streets.

The shop was in the business district in downtown Zurich, so there were many men going to and from work dressed in suits and business casual attire. I really liked imagining what each one of their jobs were or trying to decide what they were going to do at work today.

A black Mercedes SUV was illegally parked right in front of where I was sitting. I imagined that it belonged to an extremely impatient CEO of a banking firm in the office building beside the coffee shop. He would rather pay the parking fine then have to wait for his car each time he needed it.

I was still sitting at that table on the sidewalk an hour later when I saw him. I had been remembering a particularly good part of JP and me fucking from last night which caused me to have to shift in my chair to adjust my hard-on. The metal and glass building next to the coffee shop appeared to be a mortgage firm of some sort. It had a turnstile door which had not been very busy so far. I was watching it when it began to turn.

What appeared in the turnstile made me blink several times. The glass partition rotated open and a very large man stepped out of it. He was of particular note because he was one hundred percent my type—tall, heavyset, muscular, hairy, handsome, and masculine.

And he was completely naked as he headed for the black Mercedes.

I couldn't believe it. He was huge and hung like a fucking stallion—his cock hard and pointing straight up against his hairy belly.

"Whoa!" I said a little more loudly than I meant to.

The naked man stopped in his tracks and turned towards me. He quickly scanned the coffee shop patrons. Panicked, I quickly turned from side to side to see if the other patrons of the coffee shop were seeing what I was. No one seemed to have even noticed the man. I was amazed that not one single person was looking, laughing, or pointing at the man.

I looked back at him and he was staring right at me. The world seemed to pause—all noise was silenced and all movement was stopped. There was nothing but he and I, and the air seemed to crackle between us.

Did I want to run? Would I run if he started to walk towards me?

I didn't know the answers to those questions. I was at once terrified and stimulated like I had never been before. Time seemed to not be passing. It seemed like we were staring at each other for hours.

The suspended time gave me a chance to really drink in the sight of him. He was taller than me, which was unusual, maybe six foot four or so. He was thick, like the body of an NFL lineman, which I loved. He was handsome, with copper-colored hair cut short and matching beard and mustache. His eyes seemed to be golden and if I was going to guess his age, I would say maybe late thirties.

I had nothing against older men, in fact, I preferred them. I had always found myself attracted to older men—my father's friends, my buddies' dads, my teachers for example. I loved that they had stories to tell and that they were usually experienced. While they weren't always as energetic at fucking as the younger men, they certainly knew tricks that the others did not know.

He was muscular all over, but not like a bodybuilder. The naked man was built more like a professional athlete in a sport that demanded power over finesse. He was unusually tanned for someone who lived in Switzerland. His broad chest was covered with the same copper hair that was on his head and face. His feet were wide and well-manicured.

This man was doing nothing to help my hard-on go down. In fact, my cock hardened even more looking at him. It felt like it might explode and burst through its fleshy sleeve.

The naked god stared at me for a few more seconds before he turned on a naked heel and went to the waiting SUV. He opened the back door and stepped inside. I had not realized that there was a driver in the car.

Staring at the Mercedes, I realized that my mouth was open. The mental picture of the naked man's ass was still being shown in my head. And it was a phenomenal ass. I closed my mouth just as the back window rolled down and a hunky arm was thrust out of the hole. The arm had a smattering of rusty hair on the top side. The arm extended and then the fingers followed suit. It was a powerful arm and hand belonging to a very powerful man.

I blinked as I tried to focus on what I was seeing. Between two of his fingers was something that glittered in the sunlight. Suddenly his thick fingers opened and the shiny object fluttered to the sidewalk. The SUV pulled away from the curb in a hurry. I watched it go by me, down the street and make a sharp turn at the end.

Looking from side to side, I saw not one single person who seemed to have noticed. Taking one more look at the shiny object on the sidewalk, I decided on a plan of action and immediately began to act on it. My hard-on had mostly gone down since I was caught up in trying to figure out what was happening instead of staring at my naked dream man.

I stood up, walked out of the dining area, and swiftly made my way towards the object. "Thank you, long legs," I said to myself as I reached it in just a few strides.

I bent down and retrieved it. It was a credit card—no, it was a business card, but I had never seen any like it. It was clear and made of some material that felt like a cross between paper and plastic. I turned it over in my hands, feeling the texture and reading the words and numbers on it. I held it up to the sky so that I could see through it.

Lifting it to my nose, I breathed in deeply. I had always trusted my sense of smell, thinking it would have told me a lot about the mystery man. Surprised at the smell, I pulled the card away from my nose. He smelled like fall—specifically fresh-picked apples and cloves. I loved the smell and wondered if it was my dream man who smelled this way, or just his business cards.

The front of the card only had three words on it—*Octavian Segunda* on one line and *Zurich* centered on the line below it. The font was small and plain, but easy to read. There was nothing pretentious about it at all. The back only held a phone number printed on the bottom right-hand corner, which I assumed was a Swiss exchange.

I had never heard of Octavian Segunda before. Looking up towards my table, with some embarrassment, I realized that while the coffee patrons had not noticed Octavian at all, they sure were interested in what I was doing. I quietly slipped the card into my shorts pockets and returned to my table.

"Are you finding our country interesting?"

I looked up and saw one of the waiters standing beside me. "Very."

"May I get you something else, sir?"

"Did you see the man walk to that black car a minute ago?"

"I saw the car idling there on the street."

"But you didn't see the man?"

"No, I'm sorry. I didn't. Would you like another espresso?"

"I'll take an Americano to go, please."

Normally I would stay and drink my coffee hot while I googled Octavian Segunda on my phone, but I was completely wound up from what had just happened. All I wanted to do was go back to my hotel room and jack-off as I remembered the whole event.

CHAPTER FOUR

Excerpt from the journal of Jackson Jurgovan.

June 11, 2019

Zurich, Switzerland

The most amazing thing just happened to me . . .

He was everything that I like in a man. He was perfect for me. I could not have pieced a man together better than he was already put together. My cock is getting hard even as I write this.

His name is Octavian Segunda and his business card is the most unusual one that I have ever seen. I hope that is a sign that he is creative and successful in whatever business he is in.

Imagine the nerve and confidence that the man must have had to be able to walk completely naked out of an office building onto a downtown sidewalk in the city. He has balls for days . . .

I want to call the phone number, but I don't want this little fantasy that I am enjoying so much to end just yet. I know that just as soon as I call him, I will arrange to see him and he will fuck me and then I will be over him and I don't want to be over him just yet . . .

I got back to the hotel room and had to whack off twice just thinking about him. He's having some kind of effect on me and he hasn't even spoken to me yet. I wonder what his voice would sound like . . .

I'm going to see how much I can find out about him before I even think about calling the number. I will cyberstalk him as soon as I wake up from this nap that I'm about to take. I hope to dream of my mystery man . . .

Waking up from my nap, I realized that I felt better than I had for a very long time. I couldn't help but smile into the bathroom mirror on my way to the shower.

What was the cause for this sudden rush of happiness? I knew in my heart that it was the mystery man, but why? I had always loved the chase much more than the actual sex, and this man had put on a show for me that had ignited my fire.

I showered quickly and threw on one of the hotel robes. It was too small for me, but I left the front open anyway. I sat down on the sofa and pulled my laptop onto my legs. Now I would get to see the flaws of my fantasy man—ugly pictures, police records, disgruntled people blasting him on social media, bankruptcies, and his political stance that I probably would not have been able to stand.

Opening my laptop, I waited for it to power up. I had already connected to the hotel's WiFi, so the laptop went right to the internet. I typed his name into the search bar and hit enter.

Octavian Segunda came right up, so I immediately clicked on the Images tab. What appeared next had never happened to me before—not one single picture of the naked god appeared on the screen. There were some pictures of his office building, the sign for one of his businesses, and some pictures of other people with similar names, but not even a hint of a picture of him.

"What the fuck?" I tabbed back to the Everything tab and saw that there was only the webpage for his holding company and his Wikipedia page. I clicked on the link for his biography.

Octavian Segunda is a 40-year-old business man
from Romania who currently lives in Zurich, Switzerland.
He owns multiple businesses, mostly in banking
and finance and is said to be worth close to four
billion dollars. He has made most of his money by
being one or two steps ahead of the stock market
At all times. Not much is known about his personal life,
because Mr. Segunda is a recluse. It is rumored that he

suffers from a very rare skin condition. He is never seen
in public and only gives interviews by phone. He currently
has two marked men from The Service for his pleasure.
Mr. Segunda contributes heavily to charities, especially
those that help the victims of fires. He also is very
active with Romanian politics and aid.

He sounded respectable. I liked the causes that he supported and I loved that he was a successful businessman. He was worth a whole lot more than I was. Funny, I had not seen any kind of skin condition on him.

I decided to not the call the number on the card. I had never desperately chased a NOMAR before. I prided myself in being able to attract any man I wanted with them thinking they were chasing me. I was not going to let Octavian Segunda take my power away by making me come to him by just dropping his business card on the sidewalk.

I was terrified by this man and fascinated by him at the same time. Octavian was exactly my type of man and one of the most handsome men that I had ever seen in person. I didn't want to rush into this like I usually did. I didn't want to blow this opportunity. I wanted to blow him, but not the chance fate had given me.

"How could he be a recluse if he goes out in public completely naked?" I asked the air inside my hotel room.

"Why are there no pictures of that? How could there be no pictures of that?"

"What rare skin condition? He looked fine as hell to me, and he was outside in broad daylight when I saw him."

Even though I was not going to call, I was determined on action. It took me just a few minutes to find Octavian Segunda's addresses for his home and his office. I planned to observe them and learn as much as I could about the wealthy recluse.

I checked close to ten different types of social media and

found that Octavian had no presence on any of them. I shook my head in disbelief.

"Two Servants?" I asked my empty hotel room. "What kind of man has two Servants? A real man, that's who," I answered myself. "A very rich and very horny man."

I went back to the coffee shop every day for the next three days at the same time, but I never saw Octavian again. I didn't even see the black Mercedes SUV. Each afternoon, after being frustrated by not having any luck, I would have to go back to my hotel and whack one out, thinking of him. If that was his strategy to get me to call, it almost worked.

On the fourth day, I finally broke down and took a taxi to the home address that I had found for him. I left the taxi at the corner and walked down the sidewalk until I saw the address on the iron gate. I kept walking and stopped on the other side.

It was a neighborhood of huge houses in the suburbs of Zurich, and Octavian's house was the largest of the bunch. It was a long brick mansion of varying heights surrounded by a high brick and iron fence that ran around the outer edge of the grounds. Flowers and creeping vines were planted at the base of the fence, giving the whole scene a pastoral serenity.

The calm demeanor of the house was disrupted by the constant movement of quite a number of security guards. They carried weapons and patrolled the perimeter of the house and yard constantly. I assumed that the fence was electrified as well. The only other movement in the scene was that of multiple cameras posted on the outside of the house and on the gates. The cameras were constantly scanning the scene.

I crouched in a park across the street and watched the house. For close to half an hour nothing happened, not until one of the garage doors opened and the black Mercedes SUV pulled out of it.

My cock immediately got hard as I wondered if Octavian was in the back seat or not. My question went unanswered, because the SUV was too fast for me to be able to see inside the vehicle. I watched the black car move quickly into the street and away from me.

I waited ten more minutes before I decided on another plan of action. I walked through the park back to the intersection, where I used my phone to call for another taxi.

"Guten Morgen," the driver said to me as I slid into the back seat.

"Good morning," I said in English so that he would switch to my language.

"Where would you like to go?" he asked in English without hesitation.

"There's a coffee shop in the business district . . ."

A few minutes later, we were driving by my coffee shop and I saw that there was no sign of the black Mercedes. I gave the driver the address of Octavian's office as my next location.

The taxi came to a stop in front of a very strange office building—beautiful and unique. The building took up an entire block and was five stories tall. The whole building seemed to be glass, but it had a metal sculptural covering that covered every single window. The metal appeared to be copper.

I could see the genius in it right away. All of the windows let light into the building, but the dark, reflective covering kept anyone from seeing what was happening inside. There was one very small sign on the building that proclaimed it to be the offices of Octavian Segunda, but that was it.

I exited the taxi across the street and quickly walked to the back of the building. There was no sign of the Mercedes, but I did see that there was a heavily fortified ramp leading down under the building. Octavian had arranged it so that he could get into the car inside his house and exit the car under his office building so that he was never vulnerable. Smart.

I realized there was no way that I was going to be able to see him here. I caught another taxi back to the hotel and I bought a Vespa later in the afternoon. The next day, I followed the SUV from the house to a nearby gas station.

I got close enough to the car to see that no one was in the back seat, so I pulled into the pump beside the Mercedes. I pretended to get gas while I watched the driver exit and start to pump his own gas. It was curious that the car didn't have darkened windows.

The driver circled the car and went to the pump in front of me. Octavian's driver was a beast. He wore black boots, at least a size fourteen, black cargo pants, and a sleeveless black hoodie. His arms were gigantic and completely covered with tattoos, from the top of his biceps to his hands. He had a full black beard and a military haircut. Scars on his face let me know not to fuck with him, as if the rest of him hadn't told me that.

The driver caught me checking him out and gave me a head nod. I looked away immediately and completed my transaction at the pump. Looking back over my shoulder, I saw the driver still watching me. He winked at me and made sure I saw him. I gave him a cockeyed smile that tried to hide my embarrassment.

My cover was blown. Hopping on the Vespa, I sped back to my hotel room. It was only while I masturbating for the hundredth time, thinking of Octavian Segunda, that I realized that I needed to be fucked. I couldn't remember the last time I had gone so many days without a man on top of me. I vowed to go out and find me a man tonight.

After dinner at the hotel, I ordered a taxi and had it take me to a high-class nightclub with a lot of security. I had researched these clubs in each city that I was visiting well before my trip to Europe, so it was just a matter of checking my list for the one in Zurich.

This one was called Mascotte, and they had live bands, DJs, comedians, and live performance art. Located in a hundred-year-old building, the place was unique. I felt right at home as soon as I walked into it.

My presence drew a lot of attention and I didn't pay for a single drink the whole night, but I was careful to only accept them from the bartender. I never let the same guy buy more than one drink.

After an hour or so, I was bored of looking for Octavian on the dance floor. There was no one here like him. I settled for a forty-five-year-old biker with muscles and the type of shaved head that I liked. His name was Otto.

Otto had a thick dick of average length. He was so excited, once I got him back to my hotel, that he came while I blew him. I swallowed his spunk and got one good fuck from him before he collapsed exhausted onto my bed, snoring. That was the risk of being with older men sometimes.

Instead of satisfaction, all I felt was disappointment. And the worst part of all was that I couldn't get Octavian Segunda out of my head during the whole thing.

CHAPTER FIVE

Excerpt from the journal of Jackson Jurgovan.

June 15, 2019
Zurich, Switzerland
I have had a very frustrating few days. No one is measuring up to the image of Octavian Segunda, and I can't get him out of my head.

If I stay here, I will wind up calling the number on the card and surrendering all of my power to the big man. I will enjoy getting fucked by him, of course, but then the fantasy will be over . . .

I've decided to leave Zurich and see if I can clear my mind. I have purchased train tickets to Innsbruck, Austria tomorrow night.

I will probably go to his house one more time in the morning to see if I can see him, but I'm not going to put too much hope into it. I still can't believe he doesn't go outside at all. Doesn't he have a dog to walk or a multi-billion dollar merger to contemplate?

I can always come back to Zurich and call the number if I have to/want to/need to.

After my morning coffee, I was ready for my last shot at trying to intercept Octavian. I took my Vespa to his house, making sure to enter the park from the opposite end of where his house was located. I left my ride chained to a tree in the park while I walked to the section across the street from his house. I took up my spot across the house and waited.

I had brought a croissant and some cheese with me, so I slowly began to munch on those as I watched the house. I chided myself for being so passive with this man. I knew that I wanted him to come to me, but what I was doing was ridiculous. Never should a NOMAR have such an effect on a marked man, and I was feeding right into it.

An hour passed with absolutely no movement in the house or yard, save for the constantly patrolling security guards. I leaned against the trunk of a tree and tried to imagine what the inside of each room looked like. I didn't know Octavian well enough to know his style, so it was a total guess — bedroom was definitely recluse chic, kitchen was modern stainless steel, formal dining room with chair railing and chandelier, and man's cave for the den.

Nothing seemed to be happening at the house and my guessing game was over, so I was just starting to wonder if I should just go when something amazing happened. I had been so intently watching the house that I did not notice while something brown rose into the air beside me. The striking of the match certainly caught my eye.

My head snapped to the side, but there was nothing but a lit match and a cigar floating in the air beside me. I took a deep breath and smelled the unmistakable odor of freshly picked apples and clove.

He's here!

I watched in amazement as the match touched the cigar end and smoke poured out of both sides of the cigar. My cock started to swell with blood immediately. I didn't know how he was doing this little trick, but he probably had access to some kind of high-tech government cloaking device like in the movie *Predator*.

"Why are you watching me?" a deep voice asked before the match was blown out and discarded on the ground. The voice was coming from right beside me and it was so husky and deep that it sent even more pings of sexual energy straight to my balls. His voice was masculine and commanding and it told me everything I wanted to know about the way he would fuck. It was a voice that I needed to tell me what to do.

I did turn and look over my shoulder just to make sure I wasn't being pranked, but I saw nothing. Turning my whole body sideways to face where I thought he was standing, I stared hard at the bushes and grass where he should have been. My first clue was that the grass right beside me was no longer standing straight up and down. The blades were bent over and crushed.

"Well, marked man?"

"I am free to watch whomever I want, am I not?" I watched as air seemed to flow into the cigar and a puff of grey smoke came out of the end. How the hell was he doing that? And then, a brilliant flesh-colored flicker ran across the space he occupied. I got a quick glimpse of him—copper-colored hair against his tanned skin, huge fucking cock, and handsome smirking face. And then it was gone.

"You did not call the number on the card, yet you constantly watch me. It is odd."

I felt the blood rushing to my face and balls. My cock was getting harder and harder. There was a shimmer of color in front of the green bush beside me. I could see more of him now and it lasted longer.

"I've only been here once. That's hardly constant," I lied.

A puff of cigar smoke came out of the cigar. "You obviously didn't see me the other days that you were here."

Oh, fuck. "No. Did you see me?"

"Of course. I also saw you several times at that coffee shop that you like so much."

Alarm bells rang out in my head, but I was too busy getting hard to listen to them. The smell of this man was overwhelming my senses and I could now see almost all of him, although it was like he was standing in swirling smoke from his cigar. Being this close to his dick made it seem even bigger and thicker than I had remembered it. It was scary, it was so big.

He continued talking as I just stared. "And you didn't see me in your hotel room?"

"My hotel room?" I asked in shock.

The shimmer flashed faster and faster over him, allowing me to see his amazing naked body more and more. As handsome as he was, I only had eyes for his amazing cock. It was so big this close that I couldn't believe that it was real. It was rock hard and stuck straight up to heaven.

"Just long enough to browse your search history on your laptop. I didn't take anything," he said with a smirk.

"From what I read, there's nothing you need," I told him.

"Well, there was one thing . . ."

Oh, fuck. He wants me as much as I want him . . .

"You may get it yet," I said flirtatiously.

"Oh, I'm definitely going to get it," he said with swagger. "You will be mine within the hour."

The very thought of him fucking me within the hour made a movie play in my head that almost made me swoon with excitement. I loved his confidence and swagger.

Two men walked by us on the sidewalk with a dog on a leash. They both stared at me like I was some kind of pervert. Neither of them even glanced at the over-sized naked man standing beside me.

He looked at me with his head slightly tilted, like he could see right into my soul. "For a second there at the coffee shop, I thought . . ."

When I saw that he was not going to continue, I prompted him, "You thought what?"

He chuckled and said, "I thought you might have seen me. But, I can see now that I was just being foolish. You probably just found my business card and Googled me."

I saw multiple emotions cross his face — sadness, loss, fleeting hope, disappointment. This man had a very unique history and I wanted to explore it with him. His smell and his nearness were threatening to overwhelm my senses. I wasn't sure what to say, so I swallowed and just stared at him.

He shook his head like he was clearing a bad thought. "Don't you want to ask me anything, marked man?"

I looked down at his amazing feet and asked, "Isn't going out barefoot all the time hard on the soles of your feet?"

He laughed with a deep hearty sound and asked, "I come to you with something amazing, something other-worldly, something unbelievable and all you ask me about are my feet?" He took a long pull on his cigar. "And yes, it is hard on my feet."

"Well, it's not so unbelievable to see a naked man in public, although you are one helluva a naked man." I rambled on, "Your feet are extraordinary. I would not mind treating them real nice, if given the chance."

There was a pause and then I saw on his face that he was putting the pieces together. "Wait. Can you see me now?"

My dick was hard as the trunk of a tree. "Of course."

"You can see the cigar, but not me," he said quietly.

"I can see all of you including that impressive horse cock you got swinging between your legs," I answered with a smirk of my own. "Although it always seems to be hard as a rock and stuck onto your belly every time I see you out in public."

He bit the cigar between his teeth, turned to me, and grabbed me by the face with both hands. He was only slightly taller than I, so I could easily look at him face-to-face. His skin on mine made electric currents fly through my body. White bolts of energy ran to all parts of my body. I had never felt a connection to anyone like the one I already had with Octavian.

"What color are my eyes?"

"They are not exactly one color," I stalled. I was lost in his eyes and the world seemed to stop all around us. The air crackled with electricity.

"Well?" he demanded.

"Golden," I blurted out.

Suddenly the cigar dropped to the ground and he was gone. He left so quickly that I wasn't even sure which way he had gone. I picked up the cigar and examined it while my mind replayed the last part of our conversation.

What had I said that drove him away?

I thought I had him. Absentmindedly, I stroked my cheeks where had touched me with his rough hands. Most NOMARs would not have had the willpower or the desire to leave me. This man was different. Everything about him screamed that he was different from any man I had ever met before. I wanted him more than ever.

Still being afraid of him being a one-and-done, I went to my Vespa and returned to my hotel room. I was confused by what had happened, but I was still horny as fuck. There was only one thing to do — whack off while I imagined him on top of me.

I hadn't been forced to masturbate this often since I was thirteen and had just received my mark. I lay on the bed, exhausted both mentally and physically by my interaction with the big man. Calling the train station, I cancelled my ticket to Innsbruck.

I fell asleep, with my phone still in my hand and my tissues full of cum still on the side of the bed. I dreamed of a man appearing out of fog who ravished me until dawn when he disappeared with the fog.

I woke up groggy and not sure where I was. It took me a few seconds to remember what had happened the day before, but it quickly came rushing back to me.

CHAPTER SIX

Excerpt from the journal of Jackson Jurgovan.

June 16, 2019
Zurich, Switzerland
I met the most intriguing man yesterday. He is the one that I've been chasing, but he finally found me yesterday.

We stood in the park together and talked for quite a while. He is funny and commanding. He is confident and self-aware. I liked talking to him a whole lot. He would make a good Master.

Did I mention that he was invisible for the first few minutes of our talk? The longer we talked, the more of him I could see. He is even more impressive close-up. He is my kind of man. And he is the kind of man that I've always dreamed of being with.

He challenged me, asking me if I could see him. I told him that I could, and he didn't believe me. He touched me for the first time, and it felt like I was the only person in the world. His hands were rough, not what you would picture on a billionaire banker at all. His skin on mine produced electric currents like I had never felt before. Do other people feel this way? Should I have been feeling this way all along?

When I proved to Octavian that I could see him, he left me with a speed that made my head spin. I'm at a loss over what I did to upset him, but his leaving has wrecked me. I don't know what I want to do now . . .

Waking up, I stayed a little while longer in the bed, feeling sorry for myself. I still felt very tired and confused. I rolled and thrashed in the covers until my bladder threatened to release right there in the bed. My stomach was in support of my bladder, growling to let me know it wasn't happy as I relieved myself.

I forced myself to take a long hot shower. There was no way I could stop Octavian from running through my mind constantly, but at least I could look better than I felt.

Thirty minutes later, I was walking through the lobby towards my favorite coffee shop. I had dressed in my best casual clothes—a white linen shirt, blue dress shorts, and blue canvas boat shoes. I felt like shit, but I looked good.

I would not be sitting outside at the coffee shop or even staying there to drink it. I was in no mood for that. I just wanted a coffee and maybe a Danish. They could both be consumed in my room while I decided what I needed to do to get myself out of the funk that I was in, thanks to Octavian Segunda.

Leaving the hotel, I was surprised to see the black Mercedes SUV parked in the front circle. The big man that I had seen at the gas station immediately scrambled from his position of leaning on the front bumper and opened the back door as I approached. I stopped in my tracks to see if Octavian was going to exit the car.

He did not, at least that I could see. The driver stood by the door and waited for me to approach. I carefully stepped up to the big man, and he pulled an index card out of the pocket of his jacket and handed it to me.

I read it carefully.

Jackson,

Get in the car.

-8

"Fuck you, Octavian. I don't even know you. Why would I go with this man that you sent to collect me?" I didn't know if Octavian could hear me or not, but I was speaking to him like he could.

The driver pulled another index card out of his coat pocket

and handed it to me.

I read it in disbelief.

His name is Daniel. He is my driver.

Get into the car now.

8

It really annoyed me that he had anticipated my first question. "Why would I go with him, so you can just leave me again?"

Daniel smirked, pulled another card out and handed it to me.

I need to apologize to you, but I prefer to do it in private.

Get into the car.

-8

I was starting to lose my temper towards him. He was writing all the right things. I took a quick glance into the back seat and saw a tray of some sort. Daniel handed me another card.

Please. I have breakfast for you waiting in the car.

-8

"I haven't had my coffee yet," I said in weak reply. The big driver pulled yet another card out of his jacket.

It's in the car. And there is bacon . . .

-8

"Fuck me." I put my hands up onto my head and tried to think of a good reason not to get into the car. I couldn't think of one, probably because I didn't want to think of one.

I slowly climbed into the back seat of the car, trying to be careful not to disturb the tray of food beside me. Daniel shut the door and I breathed in heavily of Octavian's scent — fresh picked apples and cloves. It permeated the back seat and made my balls come alive.

The big driver went around and got behind the wheel. Closing the door and starting the engine, he finally reached back and handed me another index card.

Eat. Now.

-8

"Bossy now, aren't we?" I asked myself as I reached for some bacon. First of all, how did he know what kind of coffee I drank and secondly, how did he know I had an affinity for bacon?

The food was good and the coffee was even better. It was exactly the way that I would have ordered it, which was really unusually heavy on the cream and sugar. The bacon was super-crispy, exactly the way I liked it, as well.

"Does your boss do this often, Daniel? I mean, send you to pick up random marked men and bring them to him?"

Daniel did not turn towards me, but instead handed another index card back to me.

Daniel doesn't speak.
Save your questions for me and I will
Consider answering them when you
Are with me.
-8

My cock was rock hard. I loved the last line of that card. Fantasizing about being with him, I almost didn't notice when we pulled into the driveway of his house. Daniel stopped the car at a guard shack.

"Morning, Daniel," one of the guards said once the window rolled down.

Daniel nodded.

The guard looked into the back seat at me. "And is this the package that Mr. Segunda said you would deliver?"

Daniel nodded again.

"Please step out of the car, sir."

I opened the door and stepped outside. The guard ushered me to the back of the SUV where he patted me down, completely and thoroughly. He walked me back to the side of the car and then stepped into the guard shack to grab something black. Daniel was also out of the car now.

"He is clean," he said to Daniel. He turned back towards me and said, "Put your cellphone and wallet into this bag."

"Hell no," I said, more to Octavian than to the guard. "Octavian, you know that a marked man has to protect himself. That cellphone is my lifeline. I will not give it up."

The walkie talkie on the guard's belt came to life. It squawked, "He can keep the phone with him." It was Octavian's deep voice.

"That's not protocol, Mr. Segunda."

"If you want to keep your job, you will do as I command."

I hadn't thought my cock could get any harder, but nothing turned me on like a NOMAR that knew how to be a dominant. And Octavian Segunda was a dominant who knew how to command.

"You heard him," I said to the guard as I stepped back into the car.

Daniel started the car, but we didn't move forward at first. I was especially surprised when he handed me another index card.

This card was not written by Octavian. I assumed that it was Daniel's writing.

Be careful with the Master. He does
Not tolerate insubordination.

Insubordination? "What do you mean by insubordination, Daniel?"

He wrote something and handed me another index card. It only had one word written on it.

Disobedience

Daniel thought I was being disobedient? Or was he warning me? I was still contemplating the meaning of Daniel's card when he pulled the SUV into a garage. I reached for the door handle and found it to be locked.

I looked at Daniel in the front seat as he cut the engine and did not move. The garage door made a heavy sealing noise as it came in contact with the concrete. Immediately, Daniel moved and I heard the doors click.

Reaching for the door latch, I found that the door was un-locked. I opened it and stepped outside. The big driver bowed to me before walking through a door on the far right of the garage. At the same time, a door on the left opened and an Asian man dressed in a suit came through it.

"Hello, Mr. Jurgovan. I am Konju, Mr. Segunda's steward."

"Hello." I noticed right away that he was not marked.

"If you will kindly follow me?"

"Certainly. Your English is excellent, by the way." I stepped into a wood paneled hallway that was beautifully ap-pointed.

"Thank you. And do you speak any other languages?"

"Unfortunately, no."

"It will not matter now anyway," he told me as he ushered me into a neat office and indicated for me to take a seat.

"Why's that?"

"The Master rarely lets his Servants speak."

I sat down. "I'm not his Servant."

"A technicality, I'm sure," he said as he sat down at the desk. He handed me a clipboard with several papers on it and said, "Please complete these and ring this bell when you are finished. Do not leave this office."

I stared at him like he had two heads. "Seriously?"

"If you want to meet the Master, you will complete the pa-perwork."

"I have met him before . . . without the paperwork."

He shot me a stern look. "I can't help that, but if you want to meet with him in this house, you will comply with my in-structions." He quickly left the office before I could protest more.

I felt like saying, "Screw it," and leaving, but the lure of Octavian was just too much for me.

I started to read the first paper. One was a standard non-disclosure waiver and one was a specific ban from discussing any part of my visit, specifically security and house plans. Another form was permission for a background check. The last form, which I refused to complete, was the permission for them to give me a lie detector test.

"I'm not taking that test, Octavian," I said loudly to the air. "You've already caught me in one lie, so you know that I am a liar. Can we just say that you don't trust me and move on?"

Konju appeared at the office door.

Octavian's deep voice rang out in the office. "Konju, please escort Mr. Jurgovan to my office."

"Yes, Master." He turned to me and said, "Follow me, please."

I followed him out of the office and down another hallway. I was grateful to stand to shift the hardening dick in my pants. "How long have you been with Octavian, Konju?"

"Long enough to know that this is unusual for him."

"What is unusual?"

"The Master showing you favor."

"The Master will probably get my favor soon, if I ever get to see him."

"Don't be crass when you are with the Master," he snapped at me without breaking stride.

"I plan to be absolutely filthy when I'm with him," I said with no apologies.

The Japanese steward stopped at a set of French doors and grabbed both knobs. "I would hold my tongue, if I were you." He pulled both doors open dramatically.

"Mr. Jackson Jurgovan," he announced into the room.

I stepped into a room like I had never seen before. And it took my breath away.

CHAPTER SEVEN

Excerpt from the journal of Jackson Jurgovan.

June 16, 2019
Zurich, Switzerland
I was thrilled to see Octavian's black Mercedes in front of the hotel when I was going to get coffee this morning.

The driver, whose name is Daniel btw, opened the back door and my heart nearly stopped thinking that Octavian was going to exit the car right there in front of me.

But instead, the driver handed me a card from him. He wanted me to get into the car. I talked to Octavian like he could hear me because I wasn't sure whether he was wearing his cloaking device or not. Daniel had another card for me and then another. Octavian had anticipated my every response.

He finally won me over by telling me that he wanted to apologize to me and that he had my coffee and breakfast, including bacon, in the car. Both were exactly how I liked them. He has done some re-search . . .

I'm unsure of how he knows so much about me already, but I'm thrilled that he has made the effort. I like the direction that we are heading.

Octavian's office might have been one of the strangest rooms I had ever seen. I had expected it to look like a heavy-wooden paneled library or an ultra-modern workspace with a standing desk or something. But I did not imagine this.

His office was all glass and clear acrylic. The desk was a super-thick slab of glass with beveled edges set on glass parabolas. The lamps were all clear glass, the seats were all clear acrylic, and there was even a glass sofa with icy blue cushions on top. The bookcases were glass as were all of the book ends. A beautiful spray of fresh flowers provided color to the room, even though they sat in a crystal vase. Glass fiber strands of light fell from the ceiling like icicles and the dark wood floor was mostly covered with a swath of icy blue carpet.

The whole back wall of the office was a clear sheet of glass that allowed me to look out onto the spacious back yard. As private as Octavian seemed to be, the fact that he walked naked in public and had this wall kinda made him an exhibitionist at heart.

As amazing as the room was, what it contained was even more exciting. The whole room smelled like Octavian's musk — fresh apples and cloves. The smell went straight to my rock-hard cock and balls.

Octavian was standing in the room, off to the side. He wore a pair of basketball shorts that hung to his knees and a tight tank top. He looked like he might have stepped right off the cover of *Men's Health* magazine. The outline of his giant cock was quite evident through the silky material of his shorts. He was hard for me.

My own cock was hard as a rock, and looking at his amazing body was not helping the situation. Octavian was standing between two large aquatic tanks built into the bookcases. There were two more on my side. I wasn't sure, but I thought I saw an octopus in each instead of fish.

"Jackson," he said gruffly.

"Mr. Segunda, how nice of you to whisk me away just to have me sign over all of my rights."

"Your smart mouth will be remedied shortly."

"Why is that?"

"You will be my Servant and I will control how much you

say and when."

"I'm not here to become your Servant, Octavian."

"You are here because you want me to fuck you, aren't you?" he asked confidently.

"I am," I admitted. "But it will be a one-and-done kinda deal and I will continue my European vacation."

He laughed. "It will take me close to a month to train your ass to accept me, and then after all that, you will just leave me?"

Now it was my turn to laugh. "I'm not hanging around for a month waiting on you to fuck me, you big lug. I thought you were going to apologize to me."

The jovial smirk on his face changed to concern. "I am very sorry for leaving you the other day, but I had a very strange reaction to the fact that you are not unnerved by my invisibility."

"Well, fortunately, you came into focus for me pretty quickly."

He was more forceful with his words when he spoke next. "And you keep saying that you can see me, but no one in my whole life except my father and grandfather has been able to see me, so your lies were upsetting to me as well."

I softly said, "I can see you now, Octavian."

"I'm done playing this game, Jackson. I will fuck you and release you, if that is what you want, but I will not buy into the fact that you are special."

"You are standing between two of the Octopi tanks," I said firmly.

"You could tell that by my voice."

"You are wearing a tank top and gray basketball shorts."

"My clothing is not invisible."

"Touch yourself."

"Excuse me? I am the one that gives the orders."

I rolled my eyes. "Touch yourself and I will tell you where

you touch."

"I will enjoy spanking your ass for that eye roll once you are mine."

"And I will probably enjoy it more than you." I watched as the big man reached with one hand and carefully touched his left ear.

"Left ear," I said flatly.

"Lucky guess," he said as he removed his tank top, causing me to gape at his beautiful chest. "What about now?"

He was leaning over, touching his knee. I wondered if he had removed his shirt to make me think he was going to touch his chest or not. "Right knee."

"Shut the fuck up," he said in surprise. He immediately dropped his shorts and stood in front of me completely naked. "Now?"

He was touching just the beautiful cap of his amazing dick. "I'm not sure, let me come closer to see."

I stepped forward to him. His masculine smell hit me like a force field as I approached him. Lowering to my knees on the soft carpet, I leaned forward and placed my closed lips on the velvety soft cock head.

Suddenly, an electric charge like a bolt of lightning hit me.

"Holy fuck!" Octavian said from above me.

I leaned back and looked up to him. "Did you just feel that?"

Unexpectedly, a voice called out from the other side of the room. "Well, don't let us spoil the good time."

I turned to see two older men enter the room. They were both dressed in robes, but also wore gloves, hats, and some type of wrapping on their faces and necks.

Octavian reached down and lifted me to my feet. "Jackson, this is my father, Nicolai, and my grandfather, Julis."

"Put some clothes on, Octavian," the oldest man said.

"These are the only two people in the world that I have to

be modest around," Octavian told me as he pulled his shorts up and squeezed back into his tank.

I walked over to his two relatives and shook their hands. "I'm very pleased to meet you. Jackson Jurgovan."

"A Romanian name," Nicolai said with surprise.

"I believe so, but I don't really know much about my ancestry."

"Father, grandfather, I'm glad you came when you did. Remember me telling you that I thought he could see me?"

They nodded, but I got the impression that they also did not believe.

"Well, he can!" Octavian said with excitement.

"I don't believe it," Nicolai said firmly.

"I just tested him."

Julis added, "Is that what you call it?"

I snickered. Both of them had excellent English linguistic skills. Octavian's grandfather had an elegant accent, but his father did not. Octavian himself could have passed for an American, his English was so natural.

Octavian dug in his heels. "Test him."

"If it involves him on his knees and my cock in his mouth, I'll test him," Octavian's grandfather said.

"I like him," I said with a snicker aimed at the old man's grandson.

Octavian's father started to remove the linen wrappings from his face. His grandfather followed suit.

Octavian told me as we watched, "They have always felt the need for people to see them, but I have never felt that way. I refuse to cover myself so others are more comfortable."

"Quite handsome," I said to them once they were finished. I could tell from the flickering lines across them that I was getting ready to lose my picture of the two older men. With panic, I turned towards Octavian.

He was starting to disappear as well.

"What's wrong?" he asked when he saw my face.

"You're starting to fade."

"Hurry. Describe them," he commanded.

"You mean that you're not doing something . . ."

"Now!"

"Nicolai, you are very handsome with brown hair cut short with a military high and tight. You have a scar between your brows, but it is well-healed. Julis is a handsome bald horny bastard with a full white beard and mustache. His blue eyes are arresting."

"What do you mean that we are starting to fade?" Nicolai asked.

"I can't always see Octavian," I admitted.

"I snuck up on him last time. But you saw me the whole time?"

"No. You were invisible at first, and the more we talked, the more I could see you."

"But today, you could see me from the beginning and now I'm fading?"

"Yes," I answered, holding out my hands in exasperation.

"Your cock is limp," the grandfather said.

At first, I thought he was just making a comment about me sexually, but then it occurred to me that every time I had seen Octavian was when I was hard.

"So?" Nicolai asked.

"He was hard when we came in," Julis said.

Octavian was quick to understand. "Jackson, on your knees over here," he ordered as he dropped his shorts to the carpet again.

Normally, I would never suck off a NOMAR in a room with two others watching, but I felt completely safe here as well as the fact that I really, really wanted to suck this man's cock.

I followed his directions, using both of my hands to

encircle the root of his giant shaft as I guided the big head into my mouth. As soon as my mouth touched the soft skin of his dick, the electric surge hit me like a bolt of lightning again.

I hated that he was starting to disappear. I wanted to blow the big man while I watched how my ministrations affected him. Regardless, I felt the blood rushing to my organ and my balls tingling like crazy with sexual energy.

I sucked on Octavian hard, producing several drops of pre-cum, which I greedily sucked down my throat. This man tasted like heaven and I immediately wondered what it would be like to live with him for years. As happy as I was to finally be sucking on my dream man, I was acutely aware that I was unable to swallow very much of him. My lips barely made it half-way down his giant eggplant.

Octavian reached down and placed his palm on the side of my face. "Look at me," he commanded.

I looked up to him immediately, my mouth stretched wide around his cock.

"You like sucking on that big dick, don't you?"

I couldn't possibly talk with so much dick in my mouth, so I just hummed my satisfaction to him.

"Can you see me clearly now, Jackson?"

I pulled my mouth off of his cock, letting my wet tongue lazily blaze a trail up the bottom of his giant shaft until I was free of him. "Much better, yes."

He forcefully ordered, "Stand."

I didn't want to stop sucking him, but I wanted to obey him and make him happy, so I did as he ordered.

The Swiss billionaire reached down and enveloped my hard cock with one rough hand. He squeezed and milked my cock until I started to produce some sticky pre-cum of my own.

"You enjoyed that very much, didn't you?"

"Yes, sir."

He continued to stroke my unit. The fact that his hand was hot made me want to cum all over him while I stood there.

"Wait. You think that I can see you when I'm hard?"

"When you're both hard," Julis corrected me.

"You mean you're not using some kind of device?"

"You think we use a cloaking device like in the movies?"

I blushed. "Well, yeah."

"We don't."

I asked in disbelief, "You're just invisible sometimes?"

"All the time," Nicolai answered.

"Until I met you," Octavian said, looking at me like I was a precious piece of art from a museum.

CHAPTER EIGHT

Excerpt from the journal of Jackson Jurgovan.

June 16, 2019

At the home of Octavian Segunda, written on loose notebook paper and transcribed into his journal at a later date.

Once at the home of Octavian, I was taken to an office and asked to sign multiple legal documents. I refused a lie detector test and was finally admitted to Octavian's office.

He believes that he is invisible. And the weird thing is, so do I.

Octavian tested me to prove that I could see him. I passed the test and even got my lips on the crown of his cock, but we were interrupted by the entrance of his father and grandfather.

Octavian invited them to test me as well. They removed the wraps over their faces and I described their faces before they started to disappear.

Octavian's grandfather pointed out that my hard-on was starting to disappear also. The big man of my dreams ordered me onto my knees in front of him.

This time I gave him everything I had. Sucking on his giant cock was one of the highlights of my trip so far. He tasted so good! The only regret I had was that I was not able to suck more of his big unit inside of my mouth.

I got hard again while sucking on Octavian and could see all of them very clearly by the time he made me stop sucking on him and stand in front of him. He gave me a hand-job while his grandfather explained that I could only see them when Octavian and I were both hard.

Once I realized that they were invisible to everyone else in the world and were not using some type of cloaking device, I needed a minute to process the information.

"I will show you to your bedroom," Octavian said. "You can wash your face and compose yourself."

"My bedroom?"

"Yes. You will stay here with me for tonight."

"I have a hotel room."

"You'll be able to give me more blowjobs if you spend the night here," he said with a smirk.

I couldn't argue with that.

"You will join us for lunch and we will continue to talk."

"Yes, sir." I knew that I was adding fuel to the fire by calling him this title, but I was all for it.

"Follow me." Octavian pulled out his cell phone as he got dressed again and pressed several times on it.

"We'll see you at lunch, Jackson," Octavian's father said to me as we headed out.

The house was magnificent—cultured and clean. It was beautifully decorated with the finest rugs, furniture, and artwork. For a house of this size, I expected to see some employees, but there was absolute silence in the house.

Octavian led me upstairs, my cock still just as hard as it could be. He stopped outside a wooden door and opened it for me. I walked inside to a beautiful bedroom dominated by a king-sized bed.

"Is this where you are going to fuck me?" I asked, getting my best flirt on.

"I will fuck you wherever, whenever, and as often as I feel like it." His voice was smoldering.

I swallowed hard, unable to think of something smart to say.

"You will wash your face and take some time to process what we have said. You will change clothes for lunch."

"Change clothes? I didn't bring any clothes."

"They are in the closet. I believe they are your size or close enough."

"You constantly surprise me, Octavian."

"In a good way, I hope."

"Yes." The sexual tension between us made the air crackle with electricity.

He extended his arm with his palm side up. "I will take your cell phone now."

"Why?" I asked, suddenly defensive. "I thought you understood that I have to have a lifeline."

"It is a test to see if you trust me or not."

"Do you trust me?"

"Not yet."

I reluctantly placed my cell phone into his big hand.

He smiled and said, "I will be back to get you for lunch."

"You could stay with me."

"I can do whatever I want, Jackson. For now, I want you to do as I command."

"Yes, sir."

He smirked at me and left the room, pulling the door behind him. I went to it and tried the handle. It was locked. Octavian was certainly fastidious about his security.

Instead of splashing water on my face, I decided to take a quick shower. If Octavian and I were going to fuck tonight, I wanted to be as fresh as possible. It showed how desperate I was for him, to still want him to fuck me even after finding out that he was the invisible man.

As shocking as it was for me to learn of his invisibility, it was almost as big a surprise as the moment when I pulled out the drawer beside the sink and discovered all of my toiletries. I don't mean that Octavian had everything I needed. I mean that he had the exact same products that I used every day.

I dressed in linen pants and a silk shirt. I put a pair of black velvet loafers on my feet. I had never let myself buy clothes this expensive, even though I could afford them now. They just never seemed like a priority and I didn't think the quality really mattered until I put those clothes on my body. I had been wrong.

Lying down on the bed, I smoothed my new outfit and closed my eyes.

I woke with a start. Octavian was sitting on the side of my bed watching me.

"Hello," I said groggily.

"Sleepy head. How can you see me? You can't possibly still be hard from earlier."

"I have to pee," I explained.

The big man looked fabulous. He was wearing a cream-colored sweater with a deep v neckline that showed off some of his copper chest hair. He looked good enough to eat.

"By all means," he said as he stood and pointed me towards the bathroom.

I quickly pissed. Stumbling out of the bathroom, I said, "Sorry about that. I'm ready for lunch."

Since I had relieved myself, my boner had gone away. When I looked at Octavian all I could see were his clothes moving in thin air. "Hey, are you hard again?"

"Obviously." He grabbed my wrist and moved my hand to the front of his linen pants. His big cock was snaked down one leg and jerked when I pressed on it.

I let go of his prick, but felt mine starting to jerk awake. "Is that for me?"

"It's all going to be for you, every single inch."

"I'm already drooling." And I wasn't just talking about my mouth. Blood was rushing to my cock now like the head waters of the Mississippi River. Electrical impulses suddenly flickered over Octavian.

"I see that. Follow me."

Hopping off of the bed, I rallied after Octavian, noticing

that the flickering increased in speed and frequency. I was delighted to see that he was barefoot again. The mere sight of his masculine feet made the blood rush to my dick. In fact, I was so busy looking down at his bare feet that I didn't see Octavian stop. I ran right into the back of him.

The billionaire was solid as a rock and held me to his backside with one big hand. He had his cell phone out with the other. I heard an unlocking sound. He opened a door in the hallway and held it open for me.

His deep husky voice asked, "I like being close to you, but you know that I am always the big spoon, right?"

"God, I hope so." The fact that I was pressed against his big body made me harder than ever. His masculine smell mixed with apples and cloves made me almost cream myself.

I quickly added, "You are probably used to people running into you, aren't you?"

He screwed up his face and said, "Occupational hazard, I guess."

We walked into a beautiful dining room. The table was already set with a china service, silver service, and Baccarat crystal. The table was centered under a beautiful crystal chandelier with fresh-cut flowers everywhere.

Octavian's father and grandfather both greeted me from their chairs around the table.

"Hello again," I greeted them.

"I see that you can see us again," his grandfather announced as he pointed his fork at the bulge in my crotch.

"I can, thanks to your grandson."

"You like him that much?" Julis asked.

"Physically, he is everything I have ever wanted in a man." I watched as a look of complete satisfaction crossed Octavian's face.

"I have never had anyone like me for my looks before," Octavian said with a huge smile.

"They usually just care about that huge fucking cock," his grandfather added.

"I'm not saying that his cock isn't most of the allure. I'm just glad that I can see it coming at me!"

"I still don't believe it," Nicolai told his son.

"Father, he described your faces!" He turned to me in exasperation and said, "Sit down and eat, Jackson."

"You could have told him what we look like."

"Why don't you hold up fingers and I will tell you how many?" I offered.

"You would have a ten percent chance to guess correctly each time," Nicolai said.

"I will be correct each time and every time."

"I do love his confidence," Julis said before taking a bite of his salad.

"Fine," Nicolai conceded. He held up both hands towards me and seven fingers.

"Seven."

He put all but one finger down.

"One."

He put up nine fingers.

"Nine."

"Satisfied?" Octavian asked his father.

"I just can't believe it. There is a person outside of our family who can see us. Do you think there might be others?"

"I'm not sure," Octavian answered while scrutinizing me. "Maybe his whole family can see us." He glared at me now. "Didn't I tell you to eat?"

"Yes, sir," I replied while grabbing my salad fork and digging into the leafy greens.

"You will not do well under Octavian unless you learn to follow his commands, Jackson," Nicolai told me.

"I am only going to be under him for a short time," I answered after swallowing. The wilted greens salad with miniature pasta was unbelievably good.

"We shall see," Julis added.

I looked at Octavian and said, "Do you mind telling me why your family is invisible?"

"We are cursed."

"By the Roma, many centuries ago," his grandfather added.

"Gypsies?" I asked.

"Yes," Julis answered. "My great grandfather was cursed by a Gypsy boy when our family lived in Romania. We have all been invisible to the world since."

Romania? Again the country came up on this trip . . .

"Why did he curse you?"

"No one knows for sure, but the boy was marked, and our relative was his Master."

"Weird." I looked at the big man eating beside me.

"What?" he asked, once he caught me staring.

"I can't imagine you as a big disappearing baby." I started to snicker.

"We aren't invisible until we hit puberty, smart guy." His voice dropped to a lower octave as he said, "I'm going to enjoy when my big fat baby-maker disappears inside of you."

Fuck! Octavian Segunda certainly was the most exciting man I had ever met . . .

CHAPTER NINE

Excerpt from the journal of Jackson Jurgovan.

June 16, 2019

At the home of Octavian Segunda, written on loose notebook paper and stapled into his journal at a later date.

There is something about Octavian Segunda that has me absolutely spellbound. Yes, I know that he is everything physically that I would want in a man, but it is something more than that. I have a feeling that something unusual is happening here, between the two of us, and it has nothing to do with the fact that he and his family are actually invisible.

We came the closest to full body touching today when I ran into him in the hallway. Even though we were both dressed, I couldn't help but fantasize that we were not. He is the most alluring man that I have ever met and I think I might explode if he doesn't fuck me soon.

Lunch with his father and grandfather was interesting, if not illuminating. All three men told me stories of how their invisibility has either helped or harmed them in certain times of their lives. They don't know too much about the curse that haunts their family, but I would like to learn more.

I'm glad that lunch was light, because I'm hoping to be the dessert course for Octavian. His giant cock delights me and gives me pause at the same time. I hope that I will be able to handle it when the time comes or I will look like a fool. I have never fucked with a dick that big before . . .

"Were you able to see us through the whole lunch?"

Octavian asked me as he walked me back to my bedroom. His hand was on the small of my back and he was so close to me that I could smell him easily.

"Not the whole lunch, but your nearness is helping me get hard again."

"I do that for you?"

"You have no idea the power you have."

"I'm new to this. Marked men have only felt me before, never looked at me with lust like you do."

"Now you have the right marked man . . ."

He chuckled and said, "Grandfather was right. Your confidence is very alluring."

We reached the door to the bedroom and Octavian unlocked the door with his phone.

"Why the high security? Are we in danger?"

"We do not ever let anyone see us, as there would be a lot of questions that we could not answer." He held the door open for me.

I walked inside and immediately started taking off my clothes. "So, your staff doesn't even see you?"

"They can't, so no, they don't. Except for Konju and Daniel."

"They can see you?" I asked hopefully as my underwear hit the carpet.

"No, but they are from a long line of servants for our family. They can be trusted."

"But not me?" I asked as I spun slowly and let him get a good long look at my ass.

"Especially not you," he answered as he shut the door and began to remove his clothing.

"Is there any lube in here?"

"It's in the bathroom, but we won't need it."

"Oh, I'm gonna need it. Have you seen that big baseball bat you have between your legs?" I was salivating at the sight of his naked body.

"Jackson, we are not going to fuck. There is no way you are ready." His pants hit the carpet and I saw that he was going commando, so he was ready.

I swallowed hard and whispered, "I'm ready."

Octavian approached me and put his hands on my shoulders. Electrical currents shot through my body, right into my balls. "I will be the one that tells you when you are ready." He pushed me, and I fell back onto the bed.

My eyes widened as I watched the big man follow me onto the bed. He climbed on either side of me, his body weight making me rock side to side as he towered over me.

I spread my legs and put them onto his hips above me. He lowered himself down onto his forearms on either side of my head. He cradled my head with his rough hands as he lowered his body on top of me. His face was so close to mine and my nose was full of his scent.

"I've never met anyone like you before, Jackson."

"I feel the same way, Octavian."

He stared into my eyes. "This is so different when you can see me."

I wrapped my arms around his thick middle and pulled him even closer to me. "I see you," I whispered to him.

He lowered his head and ever so softly planted his lips onto mine.

I had rarely been kissed by a NOMAR. They normally did not want this type of intimacy and usually did not want to kiss. I was stunned, but decided in the instant to go for it.

Pressing my lips harder against his, I slightly turned my head and really kissed him. It was exhilarating. Time stopped, my heart stilled, and the air crackled with electricity.

Octavian kissed me back, hard. He crushed my lips with his as he slipped his tongue into my mouth and I returned the favor. He was such a great kisser that I wondered how much practice he had doing it. He did have two Servants.

Finally, after what seemed like an eternity of making out, Octavian lifted his head and said, "Wow!"

I snickered and repeated his one-word exclamation.

When he spoke next, his voice was husky with need. "I'm going to fuck the shit out of you." He smashed his lips back down on mine again—his beard and mustache tickling the soft skin around my lips.

I was left speechless. I wanted nothing more than that, and he apparently wanted it also.

He stopped kissing me and rose back onto his hands and knees. Octavian moved with the grace of a dancer, even though he had the body of a football player. He slid up my body until he was kneeling on either side of my shoulders. He stuck a pillow under my head and guided the tip of his giant beast to my lips.

Opening my mouth, I used my tongue to swipe the drooling head, which produced sparks as I swallowed his delicious man-honey down my throat. He nudged the back of my head while leaning forward slightly to over-emphasize his point.

Oh, I got the point, I promise.

He slid his cock into my mouth and kept going until I gagged on it in the back of my throat. I moved my hands to the base of his dick and started to blow him in earnest. Once again, I was disappointed that I couldn't get him all into my mouth, but it would give me a goal to reach, and I did like to have one of those.

My cock was as hard as it could get, so I could easily see Octavian above me as I worked him over. He was holding onto the headboard and breathing heavily. I reached up to tweak his nipple with one hand as I put pressure on the bottom vein of his dick with my tongue.

"Fuck me!" he moaned.

No, fuck me . . .

I continued to put the pressure on his over-sized cock until he erupted with his climax. Even though I had prepared for the onslaught of hot thick cum, I was surprised by how much there was. His man-juice ran out of the corners of my mouth and down the outside of my throat. I swallowed as much as I could and then spent the rest of the time licking his dick like a candy apple.

Octavian did everything big, including his climaxes. He lay down beside me on the bed on his back and pulled me towards him.

"Thank you for that, Jackson."

"My pleasure." I reached down and stroked his still-hard cock. "You look like you could go again."

"I definitely could go again, if you can," he said with a twinkle in his eye.

"I would love to, as long as you can still fuck later."

"We're not going to fuck yet, Jackson."

"Why not?"

"I already told you, it will take me like a month to get your ass ready to take my cock."

"I don't think so, sir. I'm ready to go now."

"How about you wrap those lips around my cock, and I'll inspect this asshole of yours that you have so much confidence in."

Now that I was in the heat of passion, I had complete confidence in my ass's ability to take him. I wasn't worried at all. "Your wish is my command."

"My commands will be all that you can wish for when you belong to me."

I wanted to discuss this with him further, but I had a big cock to suck. I crawled on top of him until my face was at his crotch and my legs were on either side of his shoulders. I felt his fingers on my asshole at the same time that my lips touched the soft skin of his cock. The electrical charge was released at both ends of my body.

Octavian knew his way around an ass. I could tell that by his expert finger-fucking style. Rubbing lube into my ass, he had me on the edge of climaxing constantly while he rubbed, pinched, and inserted his fingers inside me. I sucked on his big dick the whole time until he climaxed again inside my mouth.

"Jackson," he moaned behind me.

The billionaire's cum was so tasty that I couldn't help but swallow as much of it as possible. His man-juice flowed out of the sides of my mouth only to be chased by my tongue later as I cleaned him up.

"I can't get enough of that," I told him as I continued to clean up his sticky pole.

"Music to my ears."

"Well, what do you think?"

"I love how responsive your rosebud is, but I don't think it is ready for my big stick just yet."

"It's ready." I was still on all fours over him.

He pushed a finger inside me. "It just barely accepts one of my thick digits. Your ass wraps around my finger and squeezes it tight. How is it gonna take that monster down there?"

"Put in another one."

"I'm not used to taking orders from my Servants."

"I'm not one of your Servants."

"Not yet," he said as he added another finger inside me. "See how it expands to fit whatever you put in it?"

"Yes, but it has a very long way to go." He put his hand on my hard cock and started to pull.

"Don't."

"Why not? Don't you need relief?"

"I won't be able to see you if I go soft."

"You might as well. I'm going to go soft here in a minute."

"Okay."

He continued to stroke my cock as I sat on his broad chest. It only took a few seconds before I was shooting spunk all over his hairy stomach.

"Holy fuck!" I breathed heavily as I rode Octavian's chest.

"Come and lay down here on my chest," he ordered.

I moved off him and the bed. Going to the bathroom, I got a washcloth wet and returned to clean his stomach. "I'd hate to have to pull that out of your hair once it hardens."

"It will be one of your many jobs once you belong to me."

Here we go . . .

CHAPTER TEN

Excerpt from the journal of Jackson Jurgovan.

June 16, 2019

At the home of Octavian Segunda, written on loose notebook paper and stapled into his journal at a later date.

Octavian and I had our first sexual encounter today. It was even more amazing than I could have imagined, even though all I did was blow him.

His cum tastes like apples!

I think he wants me to become his Servant. And he hasn't even fucked my sweet ass yet. We are going to have to have a serious conversation soon.

I'm concerned that I am drawn to this man more than any other before, but it could be the lust talking. I'll get back to you on this one after the deed is done.

The level of security around Octavian is very upsetting to me. I mean, I know that he is invisible and that could cause all kinds of problems for him if he is found out, but I'm not sure that I could be with someone who is so paranoid and suspicious. Or even more frightening – if Octavian is not paranoid, then who is after him and how far will they go to get what they want?

I watched in amazement as the man of my dreams disappeared right in front of my eyes. The last few drops of my cum on his belly seemed to float in mid-air as I wiped it away. I took the washcloth back to the bathroom and threw it into the sink.

When I returned to the bed, Octavian was completely

invisible. I could tell he was in the same position by the indentation of the bed under him.

"Come lie here on your side," he commanded. He must have pressed down on the mattress with his hand, because I saw a depressed area form.

I lay down on my side facing away from him.

He rolled onto his side and wrapped a thick arm around my stomach. His hot body was pressed against my backside from head to foot. I reached back and pressed his cock into the crack of my ass. It was the first time that I had felt him soft, although I could tell that he was right on the edge of getting hard again.

"Octavian, I will not just be one of your Servants. One of your three Servants," I corrected myself.

"I haven't asked you to be."

"I know, but you keep saying that you want me to belong to you."

"That's what I do. I collect things."

"I'm not sure that I want to be collected."

"I usually get what I want, Jackson. And you might be too special to let go."

"I can't just be another to you."

"You would not be."

I could hear that he believed his own lie even as he said it.

"Let's fuck and be done with it," I said bluntly.

"You gonna just leave me after I give you what you want?"

I repeated his phrasing. "It's what I do. I grow tired of things."

"You won't grow tired of this," he told me as he ground his big ballpark wiener into my buns.

"I'm afraid that I will," I said softly.

"Besides, we have at least a month for me to train your asshole to open wide enough for me. We will have a lot of fun during that time."

"I'm ready now."

There was silence for quite a while. He softly touched me and moved his fingertips along my leg. "Come with me. I want to show you something."

I felt the familiar tingle in my balls that told me that my dick was going to get hard. I could feel the pulsing piece of man-sausage between my buns and I knew that Octavian was also getting hard.

I followed the big man off the bed and out of the bedroom. He didn't seem concerned that neither of us were dressed. He held his phone close to his ear.

"Rene, I am coming for a visit." Octavian's deep voice was firm and controlling. He lowered the phone.

He led me to the back of the house to a staircase. At the top was a locked door which Octavian opened with his phone.

"These are the Servant's apartments," he told me as he entered.

"And they are kept locked?"

"I will enjoy when you are unable to challenge me like this." He stopped and turned around to face me. The sight of my naked dream-man right in front of me made me absolutely speechless. "For your information, they are only locked in when we are home. Otherwise, they have free rein of the house."

I swallowed hard. When I spoke, it was in a whisper, "Aren't you afraid they will not see you?"

"Rene is blind. Joaquim knows to go to his room when I call. Follow me." He turned and walked down a hallway. He stopped at a carved wooden door which he didn't bother knocking on.

I followed him inside. It was a substantial bedroom dominated by a huge bed. There was nothing inside the bedroom that seemed personal at all and I noticed that there were no mirrors, which made sense for a blind man. It could have been a random hotel room anywhere.

There was a marked man squatting in the middle of the rug beside it. I recognized The Service Squat when I saw it — a full-body squat while you were on the balls of your feet, your legs spread wide open, your forearms resting on your thighs, and your head bowed. It was painful to perform and my body remembered the pain from it immediately.

"Master," the Servant said in a firm voice.

"Rene," he said as he shut the door behind me.

Rene was completely naked and in his late twenties, if I was guessing. He had dark hair that was cut into a longer style that was stylish. Even though he was squatting, I could tell that he was on the tall side, but super-skinny.

"You may stand, Rene. I'm sure that you can tell that I have someone with me. You may speak freely."

Rene stood up and looked at me with blank eyes. "Yes, Master. And you both are naked, I believe." He spoke with a French accent, but it was not very pronounced.

I took the time to check out his mark. It was very light blue and as thin as he was.

"We are," Octavian confirmed. "This is my friend, Jackson."

"Hello, Jackson. You are marked?"

"Hi. I am."

"American?"

"Yes."

Octavian said, "Rene has been with me for four years now, but he has decided to leave me and start spending his money."

"Good for you. Best thing I ever did."

"Oh, I assumed you were a new Servant for Mr. Segunda."

"No. I'm an independent contractor now. Mr. Segunda and I are in negotiations about what might happen."

The blind Servant turned his head towards Octavian, but

did not say anything. I thought I could read *stunned* as his expression.

Octavian said, "Jackson would like to watch while I fuck you, wouldn't you, Jackson?"

"Yes." This was obviously not my first choice, but it was the next best thing.

"Watch, Master?"

Something passed between the Servant and his Master that I didn't understand.

"Yes, Rene. I'm going to fuck you and Jackson is going to watch."

"Yes, Master," Rene said with a bow of his head.

"On the bed on all fours, Servant."

Rene did not verbally answer, but followed the directions as easily as a sighted person could have.

Octavian stepped towards the bed and spread Rene's butt cheeks with one big hand. "Do you see that, Jackson?"

I stepped closer to the bed to see.

"I'm sure most NOMARs would consider that to be a big sloppy hole that Rene has, but to me it's amazing."

I'm not sure I would have liked to hear this if I was the one in Rene's position.

Octavian continued on, "It took me close to a month and a half to get Rene's ass to open wide enough to allow me to enter him, and after that I have kept him stretched open for years."

I had never really seen my ass hole, but I knew from touching it that it was not loose and open like the one I was looking at. Rene's hole was already open like an open mouth. I started to second guess myself.

Octavian pumped lube onto his hand and began to coat his massive cock with it. "My favorite thing is to be able to step up to a hole and immediately sink my sword into it like this."

The Swiss billionaire stepped onto the bed on either side of

Rene's upturned ass, pointed his stiff rod down, and pushed it into his Servant. "Ah, there it is. I love not having to take my time, go slow, or gently ease it in."

He dipped his candle in that hot ass a few times before turning to me and asking, "Now, do you think you can do that?"

I didn't want to discuss this right here, but I was left with no choice. "I'm not sure that I can let you just sink up to the nuts in there with ease the first time, but I know that I can take you the first time and I know that my ass will remember you and each time will get easier after that," I said firmly.

Octavian continued to fuck Rene with long strokes that fully rammed his meat inside his Servant's ass. Their bodies slapped together after each thrust.

"I do love your confidence," he finally said. "And I'm happy to hear that there will be more than one fuck . . ."

Shit! I'm giving too much away to this man . . .

The sight of Octavian fucking someone with that huge prick of his was almost more than I could stand. He was so fucking hot and I could see that he was an expert at fucking. It made me want to be under him immediately.

"Notice how quiet Rene is, even when he is getting long-dicked, Jackson."

"Eh, yeah, that won't be happening for us. I am quite a moaner normally and once that big thing gets inside me, I'll probably scream."

Octavian didn't say anything as he continued to fuck Rene, but the French Servant started to laugh, which made me smile broadly at the big man on top of him.

The Swiss billionaire slammed hard into Rene and pumped his load directly into his Servant's guts. Octavian grunted with his release and seemed highly satisfied. He slapped Rene on the ass and thanked him.

"Thank you for letting me see that, Rene," I said.

"It was not me. It was the Master that allowed you to see

that."

"Either way, I thank you for your part in it."

The blind Servant nodded at me as I watched Octavian pull out of him, still hard. He reached for his phone on the nightstand and pressed the screen.

"Joaquim, I am coming over."

He put the phone down and an alarm immediately sounded.

"That is their alert that I am coming and they should be in their rooms with the doors shut," Octavian explained.

I found it all to be odd, but I knew that Octavian had to be careful with his second Servant since he could see. For the Invisible Man to worry about being seen was ironic. I guess if Joaquim saw a cell phone floating down the hallway towards him, he would be scarred for life.

"Rene, how many days do you have left before you end your Service?"

"I leave next week."

"Well, good luck to you."

"Thank you, Jackson. And good luck to you, as well."

I nodded to him, even though I knew he couldn't see it.

"Jackson, let's go," Octavian commanded. "Rene, if you need to purchase anything for your trip, please let Konju know and I will take care of it."

"Master is too kind."

"Master will miss you." Octavian and I left the French Servant's room and went across the hall to another door. He opened it and held it for me to enter.

I walked into an identical bedroom as Rene's. I noticed right away that this room also did not contain any mirrors. In the open space beside the bed, a marked man squatted. He was incredibly short and muscular—like a fireplug. He was blindfolded.

"Master," he said loudly.

"Rise, Servant."

The squatting man rose on powerful legs to a standing position. He had dark hair on his head, a hairy chest, and a very heavy five o'clock shadow on his jawline. He also was completely naked. His mark was brilliant blue and covered one whole side of his face.

"Joaquim, I have someone with me. His name is Jackson."

"Welcome, Jackson," he said to me while turning his head awkwardly to different positions. His accent was Italian and it was super-thick.

"Thank you."

Octavian continued, "Jackson would like to watch me fuck you, Joaquim."

"If it is the Master's desire . . ."

"It is."

"I am yours to command, Master."

"Yes, you are," Octavian said as he sat down on the bed and then reclined onto the pillows. "You may mount me now."

I was super-impressed that Octavian was ready to fuck again so soon, but I had come to expect nothing less from him.

"Yes, Master," Joaquim said as he hurried to the bed and straddled the large frame of Octavian. He did all of this without seeing anything, which only went to show me that he had done it many times before.

The billionaire held his Servant's ass cheeks apart as Joaquim guided Octavian's massive missile into his ass hole. Joaquim had a large muscular bubble butt that was just begging to be fucked.

"Joaquim came to me earlier this year with a lot of experience," Octavian told me.

"I was quite the whore," Joaquim added.

"But it still took almost two months for him to be able to take me. He loves having his hole stretched open and being full of me, don't you?"

"Love it." The Italian Servant slowly lowered himself down Octavian's big donkey dick until he was sitting on his lap. His hole seemed to be spread to the absolute limit, and I cringed in spite of myself.

"Well, Jackson?" Octavian's deep voice brought me out of my head.

"Looks like you have him well trained, sir."

He made a scoffing sound. "You bet I do."

Octavian spun his Servant around so that he was facing me and then pulled him back onto his chest. In this position, I could see the true expansiveness of my dream man's dick as it slid back and forth into that tight asshole.

"Does Jackson want to fuck me next, Master?"

Octavian raised an eyebrow in my direction.

"I'm marked, like you."

"So, you would or wouldn't?"

"I would love to, of course, but after witnessing this, I'm afraid you wouldn't even feel me fucking you."

"No one compares to the Master," the Italian answered immediately.

"I'll have to keep that in mind," I said as I watched his hole being destroyed by the very thing that I was craving.

Chapter Eleven

Excerpt from the journal of Jackson Jurgovan.

June 16, 2019

At the home of Octavian Segunda, written in a new journal supplied by the Invisible Man himself.

I watched Octavian fuck both of his Servants today. Neither of them have ever seen him. The fucks were like viewing fine works of art. He is a master at fucking and while he wanted me to watch so that I would agree to spend months with him, all it did was make me want him even more than before. I am definitely ready to be underneath this man . . .

His first Servant, Rene, has been with him for four years and only has one week left before his Service ends. The other one, Joaquim, has just been with him for a half a year.

Octavian told Joaquim that we would be out of town for a while. He told him that he can have the run of the house and that if he goes into the city, to always take security with him.

I wonder where Octavian is going and if he is taking me or not. I'm also wondering why it matters so much to me. I'm falling for him and I haven't even fucked him yet.

The Alps were majestic and still snow-covered as they passed by our train window. Octavian had his own private railway car that he'd had connected to a long-distance train with one phone call.

"Where are we headed?" I asked as I continued to run my tongue up and down Octavian's hot cock. He had told me that he would tell me once we were in motion. His crotch smelled like fresh apples with a hint of clove and his cum tasted like the best apple strudel I had ever had.

"St. Moritz. Do you know it?"

"Site of two Winter Olympic Games. I heard it's beautiful." Using my thumb, I put pressure on the big vein running along the bottom side of his cock until another golden drop of cum welled up to the surface. I immediately licked it off of him.

"I have a chalet there. I think you might like it."

"I like this train." Octavian's passenger car was heavily fortified. Steel doors were locked from the inside and each window had lead shutters that only would rise when the train was in motion. Each window shade had an etching of an octopus with very twisted arms. The body of the octopus made the shape of an *O* and the arms each made the shape of an *S*. As far as logos went, it was well done.

"You like that you can suck my dick while we are travelling."

"I'm sure that you like that also."

"I do. Why don't you come up here and look at the scenery with me?"

"I would rather keep sucking on this big cock of yours."

"We have plenty of time for that."

"Or even better, I could ride that cock while I look out the windows?" I phrased it as a question, even though I hadn't meant it as one.

"Not yet, Jackson, not yet."

I let go of my favorite body part of his and crawled up to where I could lie across his chest. "I love that you can reload so quickly."

"Shame that the trip is so short." He put a giant hand around me and rested it on my side. His body heated mine immediately, even in the air-conditioned train car.

I laughed. "Have you always been this sexual?"

"Yes. I remember fucking my father's Servant well before

my father even thought that I should be. It was like an urge that hit me early on and it totally consumed me for a while."

"But not now?" I asked as I stroked his curly chest hair with one lazy finger.

"You have awakened something in me."

I smiled where he couldn't see it. "Oh, yeah?"

Octavian finally admitted, "I have enjoyed our little chase."

"Speaking of which, why did you assume that I would come with you on this trip?"

"Why would you not?"

"You know that all I want to do is get fucked by you, maybe a couple of times, and then I will move on." I loved the way that his chest moved up and down with each breath.

"That is what I am afraid of, but since we have not fucked, I was pretty confident that you would join me in St. Moritz."

"On the off-chance we do?"

"Exactly."

I admitted, "It is worth the chance."

"Oh, it will be." Octavian reached down and pulled me further up until our heads were beside each other. He immediately rolled me onto my back and used his knee to separate my legs while he loomed large over me on all fours. Moving between my parted legs, he used his thighs to raise my legs around his hips and waist.

We were in the most dominant position for fucking. Was he going to do it? My heart raced at just the thought that it might happen.

He held us there for a minute, locked in place. His gigantic hot boner throbbed against my stomach. I ran my hands up his popping biceps as they anchored his body above mine.

I breathed in deeply of his masculine smell. "I want you so badly," I whispered.

"If I thought it would change your mind about leaving me once I fuck you, I would impale you on my pole right now."

"It might," I lied.

He narrowed his eyes. "You don't believe that."

I felt my face fall. "I don't."

He suddenly smiled at me. "What?"

"Nothing."

"Something. Tell."

"I'm just not used to this."

"This what?"

"Sharing how I feel with you. Looking at you and trying to figure out what you are thinking. And most disturbing of all is having you look at me and really see me."

"You are quite something to look at, sir."

He growled and said, "You are so going to get the fucking that you deserve."

"I hope so," I said with relief.

"I've never had anyone like me for anything other than my dick before. The way you look at me . . ."

"You are like my perfect man . . ."

He crushed my lips with his, kissing me so passionately that I was taken off guard again. He was at once powerful and then tender as we kissed. I was completely blown away by him and when he finally rose back above me, I was left with my eyes still closed and my lips still puckered.

"You are amazing," he told me.

"I'm just here for the ride, hopefully on that huge cock of yours."

I watched his face fall. "This is just an experience for you?"

I took a deep breath and tried, without much success, to look away from his eyes. "I'm not opposed to something more, but I know myself."

"Well, we will have a lovely three or four days in St. Moritz to remember it by."

I had never been able to sustain a relationship with a man after fucking him for four days. I fucked and I moved on. This would be another hollow relationship like the one I'd had with my former Master. I would do it, of course, because I wanted him more than any other.

"It will be great," I told him. "May I suck that beautiful dick of yours again, sir?"

"Absolutely." He rolled us over so that he was on his back and I was on all fours above him. "The mountains are particularly magnificent here in the valley below St. Moritz. I don't want you to miss them."

"I can lie down on you and do both."

He rubbed my hair and said, "Perfect, but I'm going to make sure you get yours also." Octavian lifted my legs and forced me onto my knees on either side of his broad chest. He stuck his fingers inside his mouth and I heard him sucking on them.

Just as my tongue made contact with the Invisible Man's big cock, his fingers pushed through my anal ring into my ass. It wasn't his over-sized dick, but his fingers were meaty and he sure knew what he was doing.

We kept time with each other—Octavian finger fucking me at the same speed that I blew him until we both reached our release. His hot hand was on my hard cock pumping it until I shot my load all over his hairy chest and stomach. He came almost at the same time, shooting his load down my throat with the extra running down his rod and pooling at the base.

"Fuuuucccckkkkk!" Octavian moaned.

I continued to lick, pump, and suck on him. I forced more drops of cum to the surface of his pee hole which I quickly flicked off with my tongue. I couldn't get enough of him.

Finally pulling my mouth away from his hot skin, I said, "You were right. The mountains are magnificent."

"I thought you might like them."

"There was one Matterhorn in particular that I wanted to climb."

"Are you sure? It can be pretty dangerous for a novice to climb the Matterhorn."

I laughed. "I'm hardly a novice."

"But, you have never scaled the likes of this mountain before."

"I seem to turn it into a volcano every time I try."

Now it was his turn to laugh. "Yes, you do."

CHAPTER TWELVE

Excerpt from the journal of Jackson Jurgovan.

June 17, 2019

In the private railway car of Octavian Segunda on the way to St. Moritz.

The Alps are amazingly beautiful. The most spectacular sight I think I have ever seen. The rivers are overflowing with the melting snow run-off and the fields are vibrant green against the grey mountains.

Something is happening between Octavian and me. And it is not just the sex, which so far is mind-blowing. He is talking about us as partners, although I would want to be his sub more than anything if we were to stay together.

I'm starting to hope that Octavian is the man for me. I know that I will only wind up disappointed, but I can't help myself. He is everything I dream about in a man and has complete control over me, which is very exciting. The fact that I am the only person outside of his family that can see him might be the very reason for me to stick around.

The train is pulling into the station now, so I'm anxious to see the town. I'll write more later.

St. Moritz might have been the most beautiful place I had ever seen. But it took me quite a while to see it. The train pulled into the station and stopped. I wasn't able to see anything yet, because Octavian had closed the heavy lead window shutters.

"How will this work?" I asked him. Since I had ejaculated,

I had not been able to see the big man that I was lusting after. I hoped he was in the same place that I was speaking to.

"They will unload the rest of the train first and then we will leave. I will have to go completely naked without carrying anything so that they can't see me. You will have to carry our bag and get the car."

"I'm supposed to carry all of this?" I asked while holding my hands out to our luggage.

"No, I've made arrangements to have all of that taken to the chalet. You will just take that one bag with our passports, wallets, and electronics in it."

"Oh. This takes some planning out, doesn't it?"

I pictured Octavian shrugging his big shoulders as he said, "I have had to do it my whole life, so it is just second-nature for me."

"Where do I tell the driver to take us?"

"Tell him to go to the Mirage."

"The Mirage?" I asked with a raised eyebrow. "You're kidding."

"I don't kid, Jackson."

"Your little chalet has its own name?"

"It might not be as small as I portrayed it."

"I wish I could see your face."

"I'm glad that you can't. When we leave, do not talk to me or move out of the way for me or anything like that. It will give us away."

"Okay."

"It will be harder than it sounds."

"Speaking of harder than it sounds . . ." I tried to reach out for his cock, but all I got was empty air.

"Not now, Jackson. Get ready to go."

"Yes, sir." I dressed quickly and made sure all of our stuff was in the one bag that I was to carry.

"Ready?" Octavian asked from near the door.

"Ready."

The heavy iron door was opened with a shwooshing sound. I stepped out onto the platform and walked towards the station. The scene that unfolded in front of me was like a fine work of art. The train station was open at the end that overlooked the lake. I approached it in awe.

As I got to the wooden railing at the end of the terminal, I looked out over the lake surrounded by snow-capped mountains, pine trees, and chalets. It was a scene that I had only seen on TV. There was a section of bigger buildings, but it was absolutely pristine and beautiful. A spillway to the left of me provided a beautiful photo op, so I dug for my phone and started snapping pics.

"May we go now?" Octavian's deep voice whispered to me.

I looked around and saw that all of the passengers were gone from the tracks and I didn't see any of the train staff.

"Yes. It's absolutely beautiful here." I started to walk towards the station. "Do we need to buy any supplies in that store there?"

"No. The car should be on the other side of the station."

I walked around the store and into the station office. It had large glass doors that opened automatically. I said hello to the station attendant and exited the building through another glass door. I figured that Octavian would have to always go through the doors with me or they would look like they are opening on their own.

Turning to my left, I saw a line of cars. There didn't seem to be a subway or taxis anywhere nearby. I headed towards the cars. As I approached, the driver's side door opened on one of the cars and a man stepped out—Daniel, Octavian's driver.

What the fuck was he doing here?

I approached and greeted him, "Hello, Daniel."

He reached into his jacket and pulled out a card which he

handed me. It was written in his hand. *Hello, Jackson.* He opened the back door and I slid inside. Daniel held the door longer than was necessary for me to get into the car. He obviously was experienced at this.

I felt Octavian enter the car after I did. The seat cushion beside me depressed and a waft of fresh-picked apples blew into the back seat. A large invisible hand rested on my thigh closest to him.

The unmistakable tingling in my balls told me that I was going to be hard in just a moment. I'm not sure if it was his closeness to me, his smell, his hand on my thigh, or the heat pouring off of him, but he was definitely making his presence known to my body.

Octavian appeared before me in swatches of light as my dick hardened. It was hard to take my eyes off of the scenery outside to notice him appearing, but that's how hot he was, that he could compete with the Alps. St. Moritz was a sleepy little village nestled around a beautiful lake framed by huge snow-covered mountains. The road on which Daniel drove us was a winding, zigzag, back and forth ordeal up the mountains above the main part of the city center.

I saw signs for the Olympic bobsled center, and the retail stores became more glamorous the higher we climbed the mountainside. My sight of Octavian was fully realized by the time we were half-way up the mountain.

"Well, hello, there," I said to him as I watched the last of his naked form come into view.

"I see that you can see me now," he said playfully as his hand tweaked my hard boner through my pants.

"You look amazing, as usual."

"Do you like St. Moritz, Jackson?"

"It's beautiful. Breath-taking."

"When we get to the chalet, I will want you on the bed almost immediately."

It had not escaped my notice that Daniel had continued to drive the car up the mountain, far past most of the houses and stores. "Are we finally going to fuck?" I asked with surprise in my voice.

"Daniel is going to fuck you for me."

I turned to gauge his expression since I was at a loss for words, but he continued to look out of the window and ignore me.

"Daniel?"

"Yes, Daniel. He will prepare you, and if I find the fuck satisfactory, I may be convinced to fuck you myself."

"If you find it satisfactory?" My skills had never been referred to as *satisfactory* before.

He turned towards me and said, "If you are unable to take me and you are dead set on leaving me behind after a few days, then there will be no point in getting excited." His face carried the emotions that his words lacked, but I was having a hard time reading them—concern, resignation, disappointment.

"Then I will give Daniel a fuck that hopefully you will find satisfactory, sir."

Octavian flashed me a huge, beautiful smile.

Suddenly, I blurted out, "What do you do about the dentist?"

"What?"

"I'm just curious about how you go to the dentist . . . or the doctor for that matter."

"That's what you want to know about me?"

"I want to know everything about you."

He stared into my eyes for a very long time before answering. "It is one of the few times that I allow myself to be bandaged like my father and grandfather. It is not comfortable for me."

"But even when you open your mouth, he doesn't see your

teeth?"

"No. He has signed a non-disclosure agreement for his silence just like all my doctors."

Daniel had pulled the car in front of a huge house. There was a sign near the mailbox announcing it as *The Mirage*. The house was gated, but Daniel pressed a button on the dashboard that opened a huge gate for us. He drove us inside and stopped in front of the entryway.

I stepped out of the car and noticed that there were no other houses anywhere near us. We were alone on top of the mountain, looking down on everyone else. The chalet behind the gate was even more monstrous in size than I had first thought.

"Nothing but the best for Octavian Segunda."

"And his Servants."

"Of course. Their comfort level is derived from the Master's."

"Then let us go see what comforts you may like, Jackson." He extended his hand towards the open gate.

"Let's." I headed towards the gate, and, once through it, saw the magnificent summer home in all of its glory. The yard was small, but beautifully manicured. The sloping red tile roofs made the chalet look small, but I saw that there were levels built into the mountainside.

"Stunning," I said to Octavian. "I bet this always impresses the marked men you bring here."

"You are the first, Jackson."

"I'm honored."

"You have no idea how honored you will be, if you decide to stay with me."

"You spoil me, sir."

"I will spoil you like you can't imagine ..." We had reached the front door and Octavian punched a security code into a panel on the wall.

He opened the door and said, "Welcome to The Mirage,

Jackson."

I stepped into the chalet and marveled at the view. The whole side of the house that looked out over the lake was glass. The furniture inside the house looked like antique, but of really fine quality. Hardwood floors were covered by rugs and large wooden beams were carved with Swiss symbols and flowers.

"It's beautiful, Octavian."

"Thank you. I wish that I could spend more time here."

I walked through the kitchen and living room towards the glass wall. Beyond it was a cement balcony with an outdoor kitchen which even included a brick pizza oven. I could tell that the balcony had multiple levels and the most amazing views of St. Moritz that were available.

"Would you like something to eat or drink?"

I was having a hard time not looking at the view. "You sure know how to sweep a guy off his feet, Octavian."

"You will be on your back with your feet in the air shortly, Jackson. I'm going to have some wine and I suggest you do as well."

"Do you have champagne?"

"Of course."

"With strawberries?"

"Your wish is my command."

"If only that were true," I said, flashing him a huge smile.

"You are not mine to control, yet, Jackson."

The image in my mind of being under his control at once terrified and excited me beyond words.

Chapter Thirteen

Excerpt from the journal of Jackson Jurgovan.

June 18, 2019

At the summer home of Octavian Segunda in St. Moritz.

We finally arrived at St. Moritz and it was the most beautiful place I have ever seen.

Octavian's chalet is more like a mansion built into the side of the mountain. There was no other house in St. Moritz that compared to it.

He told me that I was the first marked man that he has brought here and that made me feel special. I'm not sure what plans he has for me or for us, but I am hopeful that I will be able to stay with him until I tire of him.

I was surprised to see Octavian's driver, Daniel, here when we arrived and even more surprised to learn that he will be fucking me as a trial to see if Octavian was interested.

I was not opposed to letting Daniel fuck me, but I thought it was unnecessary. I just want to be with the big man. But, if he needs to see this first, then I will jump through the hoops for him.

I have not seen any servants in the chalet so far, but we did have a wonderful dinner of sausages and beef soup waiting on us when we arrived. It probably was the same set-up here as in Zurich where he does not allow the servants to be able to see him . . . or not see him.

The very thought that I might be fucking with Octavian in the very near future gave me all the hope that I needed. I will jump through his hoops for that hope any day.

After we finished our glasses of wine, Octavian and I took a shower together. I had blown him twice by the time we made our way to the giant king-sized bed.

"Daniel!" Octavian called as he propped his head up on several pillows against the head board.

The big bodyguard appeared in the doorway. He dug in his pocket and produced a card.

Yes, Boss?

"Jackson and I will be taking a quick nap, and when we wake, he will be ready to be fucked."

Octavian's bodyguard cleverly used his over-sized thumb to cover the question mark on the card.

Yes, Boss.

"And Daniel?"

Yes, Boss. He flashed the card again.

"I need you to be at your best."

He grinned broadly and gave me a big thumbs-up. The sheer size of the man was intimidating, but I was determined to show him and Octavian what I could do. I found myself grinning foolishly back to him and giving him a thumbs-up of my own.

I fell asleep almost instantly, nestled against Octavian's hairy chest. He slept on his back and me on my side, so once again it was a sign that we fit together well.

Waking with a start, I realized that Octavian was lightly touching me along my thigh. It was disturbing to not be able to see him, but I settled down once I knew what was happening. I had not gotten used to the fact that I would not always be able to see him.

"Hi."

"Are you ready, Jackson?"

"I just woke up, but I'm always ready for a rowel."

There was silence from his side of the bed and I was unable to see his face to try to judge what he was thinking. I had always been really good at reading people's expressions and guiding the conversation based on those expressions, so this deal with Octavian was very unnerving to me.

"I am drawn to you."

Octavian's simple statement from his invisible state was a bombshell. "Because I can see you . . . sometimes?"

"I'm not sure that is all of it . . ."

"Why, then?"

"I'm not sure. You are a mystery to me, but one that I intend on solving. And soon."

"Well, that is comforting to me that at least I will be able to hold your interest for at least a little while."

"You seem to have already captivated me, despite not allowing me to fuck you yet."

"Not *allowing*?" I said with heat.

A chuckle floated from where his head should have been. "Daniel!"

The driver appeared so quickly that he must have been waiting right outside the door. He produced a card from his jacket. *Yes, boss?*

"It's time, big man."

I felt Octavian leave the bed, although I couldn't see him do it. I was naked already, but I needed to use the restroom. "I'll be right back."

Daniel was stripping even as I was heading to the restroom. I splashed water on my face and took a piss before smearing lube inside my ass. I washed my hands and looked at myself in the mirror. Taking a few deep breaths, I returned to the bedroom.

Daniel was waiting for me, standing at the bottom of the bed. He was naked and huge all over. I couldn't see Octavian in the room, but I could smell that he was still there. The driver's cock was not nearly as long or thick as Octavian's, but it did give me pause. It was bigger than most. Daniel's thick chest was covered in black hair, as were his arms, legs, back, and ass.

I knelt in front of him as he stood and let him slide his semi-hard cock into my mouth. His skin was hot on my lips and tongue and he smelled like lavender soap. I began to give him a world-class blowjob and soon found myself really into it. The bodyguard got fully hard in less than a minute.

He presented me with a card seconds later.

On the bed on all fours, Jackson

I stood and climbed onto the bed, noticing that Daniel had laid several stacks of his index cards on the sides of the bed. I was intrigued right away with whether some of them were good and some of them were not. I got on my hands and knees in the middle of the bed, trying to make sure that I did not disturb Daniel's piles of cards.

Daniel placed his big hands on my ass cheeks and separated them. Surprisingly, he used a washcloth to wipe away the lube that I had already applied. His bearded face immediately planted between my separated ass cheeks. Rarely had a NOMAR rimmed me before, and I had not been expecting it now, so instinctively my body lurched forward to escape.

The big bodyguard held me firmly in his grasp as his beard scraped my sensitive skin and licked my butthole. He grunted as he repositioned his grip and held me tighter.

I moaned with wild abandon as Daniel pushed his tongue inside me and began to spread my anal ring apart. He had done this before—there was no doubt about that. He stopped as suddenly as he had started so that he could present me with another card.

Nice ass, Jackson.

This time I saw him hold the card up to the chair on the left of the bed after I read it. I was positive that he was reporting to Octavian, so that must have been where the billionaire was sitting.

Cold liquid ran down the crack of my ass. Daniel spit into the lube that he had squirted on me and pushed the splooge directly into my hole with his finger. He pumped his thick digit back and forth as I groaned my pleasure to him. He added another finger and then more lube before I received another card.

Very tight, very small hole, Jackson. I'm not sure you will be able to take me.

"Oh, I can take you, big man. You will be pleasantly surprised, but if you're not you can always take advantage of the other marked men who are here, if you don't find me acceptable," I said with some heat.

"Jackson." Octavian's tone told me that I needed to settle down without him having to say it.

Daniel added another finger and started to saw them back and forth. He was not as skilled at finger-fucking as his boss, but I was in no position to complain about his skills.

Another card appeared to the side of me. *You ready, Jackson?*

"Ready."

I felt Daniel climb onto the bed before he spread my legs further apart with his thighs. Heat poured off his cock head right onto my rosebud. With more than a little power, he grabbed my hips and pushed his forward at the same time — feeding his big cock into me.

I closed my eyes as my asshole was spread apart to allow Daniel's dick entry. I controlled my breathing as pain shot through me from ass to brain. The pain was sharp, like a fine-honed blade slicing through me. I had learned at The Service Academy how to deal with it until the pain turned to pleasure. Most men didn't give me such pain, but Daniel and his boss were not most men.

The feel of a card against my face made me open my eyes. *Nice tight hole, Jackson.*

"Nice big dick, Daniel."

"Too tight?" Octavian's deep voice materialized out of thin air.

Daniel held up another card where I could read it before he flashed it at the chair to the side of the bed.

Like a virgin.

"He doesn't act like a virgin," Octavian said from across the room.

Octavian's bodyguard started to fuck, and all I could do was hang my head and let him do his business. He was a good fucker and had me panting in no time flat.

His ass is milking my cock like a machine.

I wanted to put on a show for Octavian, so I started to push my hips back to meet his thrusts. Daniel stopped moving and let me take over the fuck. I moved back and forth as fast as I could. I knew that Octavian was watching and I was determined to show him what I could do. I never had to audition for a NOMAR before and it made me feel many different emotions — excitement, fear, hope, anxiety, and a sense of purpose.

So fucking good.

Daniel took back over and finished himself off. He came with a roar from deep in his chest as he spewed his hot spunk in my ass. I was surprised again to hear a sound from him. He was breathing hard as he collapsed on top of my back, knocking me to the mattress.

"Well, Daniel?" Octavian asked impatiently.

Daniel took his time looking through his cards until he finally held one up for us to see.

Might be the best I've ever had.

"Seriously?"

Daniel lifted off of me, pulled his sloppy cock out of my sore hole, and grabbed another card.

Can I go again, Master?

Octavian's deep voice boomed inside the bedroom. "Sure, Daniel. Get him nice and loose and I will give him the shot he desires."

Did he just say what I think he did? He's going to give me a shot?

My dick started to harden in response to the mental picture I had of Octavian on top of me.

One shot. That was all I needed.

Chapter Fourteen

Excerpt from the journal of Jackson Jurgovan.

June 18, 2019

At the summer home of Octavian Segunda in St. Moritz.

Daniel and I fucked and it was pretty awesome. He liked it so much that he asked for another and was granted it by Octavian. He fucked me the second time by planking on top of me and fucking straight down into my up-turned ass. It was pretty hot from the big man.

Octavian must have liked my show also, because he said that he was going to give me a shot himself. However, I got hard jerking my own cock while Daniel was fucking down into me, and I was so disappointed that, once hard, I still could not see Octavian. He must have left the bedroom sometime after the second fuck started. I hoped he was not mad with me.

I spent a long time in the shower after Daniel's fuck, getting clean. I wasn't sure if Octavian would immediately want me or not, but if he did, I wanted to be ready. I debated whether to leave the bodyguard's cum in my ass to help lube me for his boss, but I decided in the end to come clean.

Once I dried off and looked presentable again, I went back into the bedroom, but it was empty. I found Octavian having another glass of wine in the living room. I wasn't hard, so all I could see was a floating glass of red wine. I took a seat on a couch across from him, making sure not to sit where my ass would hurt from the pounding that Daniel had just given me.

He greeted me and told me that I smelled fresh and clean.

I told him how beautiful the nighttime view of St. Moritz was from his house.

He nodded and took another sip of his wine.

I asked him if I had disappointed him in some way.

He promised me that I had not, but said that he had a lot on his mind.

He informed me that Daniel was leaving to see his parents, who lived nearby, and that he would be spending the night with them.

Octavian seemed sleepy rather than horny . . .

I fell asleep on Octavian's chest, riding the waves of his breathing until I was in a deep slumber. I don't think I even stirred once, until he woke me.

"Jackson, it's time."

"What? What time is it?" I could see that it was still dark outside and I thought I could see that it was after five o'clock on the screen of my cell phone.

"Time for you to get everything you have asked for, Jackson."

A bolt of lightning hit my crotch with the dawning of his words. I wiped the sleep from my eyes and said, "Yes, sir!" I was excited as a little boy on Christmas morning.

Throwing the sheet off of me, I asked, "How do you want me?" My dick was starting to harden and Octavian had turned on the bedside lamp, so I was beginning to see flickers of him.

Octavian growled and said, "You are not in charge here, Jackson. I will tell you everything you need to know."

"Yes, sir." I didn't want to piss him off and ruin my chance at fucking. Otherwise, I would have told him that I was always in charge, no matter what the NOMAR thought or wanted.

His voice had softened with his next words. "I want to show you something."

I just assumed it was his dick, which I could now see was hard as a rock and bigger looking than ever. I swallowed hard in anticipation of the pain that he was going to cause me.

Surprising me, Octavian Segunda rolled out of the bed and headed towards the closet. I breathed in deeply the masculine smell he left behind in the bed. When I looked up again, he was holding a white robe out to me. It was monogrammed with Octavian's octopus on the left chest. Confused about where this was headed, I took it from him.

I watched as he reached for one of his own and began to put it on. I had never had a NOMAR want to dress me instead of fuck me, so it took me a few seconds to get on board with his plan.

He snapped his fingers to bring me out of my head.

"Sorry, sir," I stumbled as I slid off of the big bed and hastily threw on the robe. The cotton material of the robe felt like silk on my skin. It was amazing. Once I was dressed and looking at him, he held his hand out to me.

I stared at it in shock. *What was happening?*

"Take my hand, Jackson," he said, growling like a giant copper-colored bear.

Placing my hand into his, I felt how warm he was as he wrapped his fingers around mine. He headed out of the bedroom with me in tow. We walked down the hall, me behind him but still tethered to him by our hands. Octavian led me through the living room and up to the French doors in the glass wall facing the town.

I could see St. Moritz at night by the twinkling lights from the city center. Octavian dropped my hand and used both of his to open the doors and usher us through. Once outside, he closed the doors behind him.

The wind hit me almost immediately and I shivered in response. It was very cold, and I was grateful for the over-sized warm robe now. I watched Octavian as he went to the hot tub and pressed a button. It was completely dark outside, but the moon gave me just enough light to make out what was happening.

The lid of the hot tub shook and rose before folding onto itself and forming a shield wall against the glass wall of the house. There was a pale blue bulb inside the water that provided just enough light to be able to see into the crystal blue water. Octavian looked at me and pulled his robe off. He hung it on a hook on the cover.

I followed suit and was soon naked against the wind. Octavian held out his hand to me again and I immediately took it. He guided me up the stairs and into the steaming water. Walking over to an outdoor cabinet, he grabbed several things. I could see two fluffy towels that he placed on a bench to the side of the tub. He placed a wooden box on top of them.

The control panel on the tub read one hundred and four degrees. The water felt like heaven, so warm and enveloping. I loved the freezing air combined with the very hot water. I wasn't sure where to go in the big hot tub, but I knew for sure that I wanted to watch Octavian enter it, so I positioned myself in the middle.

Octavian lithely climbed the stairs, then stepped over the hot tub wall and into the water. He had the most amazing body that I had ever seen and I couldn't get enough of him. I watched as he passed me and took the seat in the middle of the back bench.

"Come sit on my lap," he commanded.

Here we go!

I sat down on his legs facing him, my cock painfully hard.

Octavian wrapped his large arms around me, warming me even more. He looked deep into my eyes and said, "The way you look at me is arresting, Jackson."

"Arresting?"

"Yes. I'm not used to anyone seeing me and not only do you see me, but you look at me like I am the only person in the world."

"That's pretty close. You are amazing."

"It is special, Jackson."

"You are special, Octavian."

He didn't say anything else, but instead crushed my lips with his. He kissed me with all of the passion of a marked man in love and I returned the kiss just as hard. We ate each other's faces for what seemed like hours as his rough hands roamed all over my body. It was another amazing experience for me with a NOMAR and it took my breath away.

The hot water swirled all over my lower half, but the heat that was being produced by Octavian's make-out session proved to be even hotter above the waterline. I freely roamed his body with my hands—squeezing his biceps, pinching his hard little nipples, running across the wet hair matted on his chest, and stroking his big cock. I was in heaven. Octavian, meanwhile, was intent to just hold my head steady while we kissed. I was sweating profusely, although I wasn't sure if it was from the heat of the water or the lust in my heart.

Finally, when he broke apart from me, we could both breathe in the crisp night air. I gulped it at first before setting down.

"Is that what you wanted me to see?"

"No, this," he answered as he put his hands on my hips and spun me around away from him.

I didn't see anything but darkness occasionally broken by the twinkling lights of St. Moritz.

He directed me, "Put your forearms on the lip of the tub in front of you."

I did as he commanded—one because he commanded it and two because it put my ass up in the middle of the hot tub which was the prime angle for it to be fucked. I was hopeful that the lube I had inserted in my asshole after my shower would not wash away in this hot tub. Thankfully, I heard Octavian jacking his cock with lube behind me.

He lifted my legs into the water and separated them.

Immediately, I felt the heat from his cock head on my asshole. I tried not to think of how big that soft beautiful glans was, but I could picture it pressing into my rosebud and I became tense anyway.

Get it together, Jackson . . .

Willing myself to relax, I picked a particular bright light from down in the valley and focused on it. Octavian seemed to be in no rush. He continued to rub his cock head up and down on my asshole and then pressed it forward. His rough hands were hot on my hips.

The billionaire continued to press his body weight behind his hard cock, but ever so slightly at a time. He had real will power, and after a few moments, all I wanted him to do was split me apart with his manhood. The pressure of his push continued to increase, but my ass had not reached its breaking point yet. The giant cock head was pressuring my ass to open to it. It felt like I was squatting over the most powerful jet in that hot tub and the water from a high-pressure nozzle was trying to enter me.

Suddenly, from across the mountains, I saw the first light of dawn as it poured through the only side of St. Moritz that wasn't surrounded by a huge cliff face. At the exact same second, Octavian Segunda pushed his giant cock inside me.

Holy fuck!

My anal ring opened further than it ever had before to accommodate the big man's hard cock. I gasped with the pain that shot straight from my ass to my brain — the feeling of being ripped apart by a hot knife as it cut me from stem to stern. I felt the panic rise up from my throat.

I'm not going to be able to do this . . .

Once his cockhead had disappeared inside me, Octavian pressed his advantage. He pushed his hips forward which drove inch after inch of his impressive member deep inside me.

Images flashed through my head — a volcano exploding

and spraying red hot lava out of it, a sinkhole opening and swallowing everything in its' path, and then something I didn't expect. My first lover appeared in my head, the boy that popped my cherry, and then the two college golfers who took turns fucking me a year later in the maintenance shed at the country club, and so on. With every inch of Octavian's cock that entered me, another one of the men who had fucked me appeared.

The pain was like nothing I had ever felt before—earth-shattering and exquisite. I held out hope that the pleasure the pain would turn into would also be the best that I had ever experienced. I realized that I was squeezing my eyes closed so hard that tears had begun to run down my face.

I willed myself to open them and take a deep breath. I had to relax, or I might never walk again. I noticed more light cutting through the darkness now. The sun was definitely rising over the mountains.

He had to be near the end, didn't he?

My ass felt so full of him and my asshole was stretched to its absolute limit. There was no way I could handle any more, but the big man behind me just kept pushing more of himself inside me. I felt like I left my body for a second and hovered over the lake and valley below me. I never had experienced anything like this before.

With a deep-chested grunt, Octavian pushed the remainder of his long fat cock inside me. He was buried up to the nuts in my ass and his short hairs tickled the sensitive skin of my butt cheeks. He let go of my hips and leaned back into the hot tub seat.

"Well, fuck me," he said with what sounded like satisfaction. "Who would have thought . . ."

I had transcended. As if God himself had forced me down onto the top of a totem pole high on a mountain. I was impaled and elevated above the world. There was no way I could have been any fuller than I was in that moment. The pain was so sharp and immediate that it left me stunned. I had left my body and was viewing the whole situation from above.

"That's a fine piece of ass," Octavian said with a growl. I heard the wooden box lid open, heard the metallic rasp of a lighter ignite, and smelled the smoke of one of his cigars. He was enjoying himself.

His normal reaction to what was happening and the smell of his cigar brought me back to myself.

"You okay, Jackson?" he asked after blowing his cigar smoke across my back.

Not trusting myself to talk just yet, I nodded to the big man behind me. The pain was still in full effect and I knew that this was just part one. Every fuck had two parts—the entrance and the pounding. If Octavian's entrance was this dramatic, I couldn't even imagine what the pounding was going to entail.

Was it possible to climb the mountain and then say you were done?

I watched the sunrise as it continued to reveal the city, lake, and mountains below me while I practiced my deep breathing. It felt like Octavian's cockhead was sitting right under my breast bone, it was so deep inside me. I had never felt this full of cock before, nor this stretched open. I was vulnerable and open to him like I had never been to any man before.

"You might be the tightest little ass I have ever been inside, Jackson. I now see what Daniel meant when he said that your ass was milking him."

I nodded my head slightly. I knew my ass was stroking the big piece of man-meat inside it by reflex and routine only. I was not in command, so my body had taken over.

"I mean, don't get me wrong, I have been with men who were so tight that they couldn't take me, but when I trained their asses, they just lose all elasticity. You are the first man that could take me without training and still be tight as a virgin on his thirteenth birthday."

When I didn't respond, he asked, "You have nothing to say, Jackson?"

I took a deep breath and once I felt like I could talk again, I asked, "Why were you hard when you came out of that office building the first time I saw you?"

"I just slid my full length all the way inside you on the first try and that is what you ask me? I must be losing my touch."

"There are not words to describe what you are doing to me right now, physically, Master."

"Master?" he asked with a shocked tone.

"You are he, Master."

"But you are not my Servant, Jackson."

"I am now. You are my true Master. I feel it in my heart, my head, and now in my guts and ass. You are the man for me." More and more of the darkness ebbed away as the sunlight filtered across the mountains.

"Is that why I am drawn to you, Jackson?"

"I believe so, Master."

There was a long pause of silence. "You want me to treat you like my Servant?"

"I want you to fuck me hard and then you can decide what to do with me."

"And you will be happy with whatever I decide?"

"I am yours to do with as you please, Master. I will be happy with you making the decision."

"Hmmm. Somehow, I find that hard to believe."

CHAPTER FIFTEEN

Excerpt from the journal of Jackson Jurgovan.

June 19, 2019- written later in the day
At the summer home of Octavian Segunda in St. Moritz.
Unbelievably Octavian Segunda has turned out to be my True Master. I have told him of this revelation and he seemed to be as surprised as I was.

I want to document the ways that I am drawn to him. It will comfort me on the day that Octavian grows tired of me.

Handsome
Older
Taller than me
Hairy, but manscaped
Smart
Good sense of humor
Dominant
Doesn't need my money
Cigar smoker
Invisible—gives us a secret that only we have
Big ass cock
Horny as hell
Fucks like a porn star
Challenges me
Values family
Smells like a real man
Makes me feel small, physically
Makes me feel safe

Hot ass
Makes me feel special
Big ass cock. Did I mention that already?

Octavian Segunda and I were in the hot tub on the balcony of his chalet in St. Moritz. He had just impaled me on his monster cock and I had just come to the realization that he was my True Master.

The feeling of fullness that I had was disturbing and exciting to me at the same time. I was so full of his cock that I felt like a puppet—his hand and his arm inside me, controlling me. When he was inside me, my body felt like an extension of his own.

I was leaning forward on the edge of the hot tub watching the sunrise over the spectacular lake and mountains of this tiny Swiss town. Octavian was leaning back, smoking a cigar. We were connected at the most base level—his cock to my ass.

"What did you want to know again?" he asked from behind me.

"I wanted to know why your cock was so hard on that first day when we saw each other, Master."

He blew out a lungful of air before he answered my question. "I had some particular good luck that day, Jackson."

So did I, Master. So did I.

"In my business, sometimes I need more information than some companies are willing to give."

"So you eavesdropped on them in your invisible state to know when to buy or sale stocks, Master?"

"Yes," his deep voice boomed from behind me. "You feel this is an invasion of their privacy?"

"I'm not torn up about it. They probably do much worse."

"Yes, if the public only knew. I justify it since I own a large number of shares invested in their businesses and I have a right to the information in a quarterly report later anyway."

I chuckled and said, "I bet you find out a lot more than is ever printed in a quarterly report."

He returned my laughter and agreed with me. There was silence while he sucked on his cigar, his cock throbbing away deep inside me, and I watched the sunrise, marveling at how he could stay so hard for so long without even a moment of hesitation.

"Why aren't you looking at me, Jackson?" he asked. "I need to see if I have dropped in your esteem."

"I don't want to . . . not see you, Master."

"What do you mean? I'm hard as a freaking fence post inside you."

"No one knows that better than me, Master, but I am soft."

"You are not turned on by my cock throbbing deep inside you, Servant?"

It was the first time he had called me by that title and it sent a cold chill up my spine despite the heat of the hot tub and the heat being thrown off by his huge dick.

"It is beyond being turned on, Master. I need your cock inside me. It is a part of me now."

"Look at me," he commanded. His voice was deep and gravelly and I could have sworn that his cock expanded inside me.

I turned to look over my shoulder. It was now light enough for me to see clearly. I saw Octavian in all of his glory — smoking and smiling at me.

"How, Master? How can I see you when one of us is not hard?"

He grinned foolishly at me. "We are one now. I can always see myself."

"I would like to watch you while you fuck the shit out of me."

"You probably want a lot of things, Jackson. One thing you must learn is that I will tell you what you are going to do and when you are going to do it, because I am your Master. I will do what I think is best for you. Do you understand?"

"Yes, Master."

"I've been waiting to let your ass get used to me being inside you, but you are still so tight. Your ass has gotten tighter around my shaft since I entered you."

"You have to fuck it open, Master. It is the only way."

"If you say so . . ." He put down his cigar and leaned forward into the tub until he was perpendicular to me. Octavian grabbed my throat with one hand, forcing my head up and back as my spine curved. He had his other hand on my hip, using it as a buffer as he pulled his big cock mostly out of me.

He slammed his big dick back inside me with power and force. I was in heaven. I closed my eyes and let my body experience every nerve cell firing with pain and every other one firing with pleasure at the feeling of being full for the first time in my life.

"Master . . ."

He pulled back out. "Yes, Servant?" He slammed back inside me.

"I am overwhelmed by you."

"I am a lot to take, but you seem to take it just fine."

He began to fuck me in stride now—putting the individual strokes back to back to make a seamless fucking motion. The experience of Octavian in full fuck mode was enough to force my eyes open and a giant deep-throated moan to escape my lips.

"Your ass is so . . . unreal," he groaned as he increased his speed and plowed my ass with gusto.

I couldn't talk anymore. I had never felt anything like this before and I was lost in him. He let go of my throat and used both hands to guide my hips back and forth over his big stick. It was hard to hang onto the side of the hot tub while my new Master was violently rocking my ass, but I did it. I gripped the side like it was a life raft and I needed to stay on it to survive.

Taking a deep breath of cold air, I could smell Master's masculine musk as he fucked me deep and hard. I imagined my asshole stretched to its maximum girth and red with irritation as it slid up and down his hard cock. My skin was on fire and my prostate screamed from being pounded to a pulp. Hopefully he wasn't doing damage to me, but the thought of stopping him from his mission made me too upset to contemplate.

The hot water in the tub sloshed around as Octavian increased his speed and fucked me like a wild bull. I ground my hips back on him after each thrust — trying to get every possible inch of him inside me. I was shamelessly whorish, but I didn't care. He was my man and I would use him for my own personal pleasure whenever I could.

My head collapsed onto my folded arms as Octavian built to his climax. He was breathing hard and grunting from the effort. His hands were slippery on my skin as the train sped towards the station.

"Fuuuuccccckkkkkk!" he roared, slamming his cock deep inside me as it exploded with his release.

I imagined that Octavian's dick head was pointed directly onto the bottom of my stomach as his cum vent opened and spewed molten hot cum directly into my bowels. The heat of his cum warmed me from the inside and made me feel even more full than before. Hot cum filled every crevice not occupied by his gigantic cock and poured out of my ass.

We were both spent — each of us breathing like we had just run a marathon. Octavian slowly pulled his still-swollen dick from me, and it made a loud popping sound as it slid out of me. He sat back onto the hot tub seat and pulled me after him. Spinning me around, he forced me down onto his lap.

"What the fuck was that?"

I whispered, "That was incredible, Master."

He cocked his head to the side and looked at me strangely. "I've never had a fuck like that before."

"Me either."

"Was it something special for you?"

I laughed, but that hurt my ass, so I stopped. "I've never, Master."

"You've never?"

"Ever."

He smiled at me as he puffed on his cigar. "You want to go again, Servant?"

"Absolutely, Master!"

"First, I want a bottle of water."

"Yeah, I could use one of those myself, Master."

He raised an eyebrow at me and asked, "Well?"

"Oh, you want me to get them, Master?"

"I expect it, Servant."

I looked at him like he might change his mind, even though my brain told me immediately that he would not.

"Why the hesitation, Servant?"

"I'm not sure I will be able to walk, Master."

"Then, by all means, take your time, Servant," he said with a smile before clamping his teeth down on the end of the cigar. "There are bottles of water in the fridge inside."

I could barely raise my legs over the side of the hot tub without the pain of a thousand hot knives lancing up my ass, but I was determined to follow Octavian's commands. Walking down the stairs of the hot tub was excruciating. Master held my robe out for me.

"Master is too kind," I said with some sarcasm in my voice as I slid into the warm garment.

"Master will spank your ass hard after he fucks it again, if he hears that tone ever again."

"Sorry, Master," I said as I made my way around the hot

tub, gingerly holding onto the side.

Slowly, I opened the French doors and stepped inside. Taking a deep breath, I moved towards the kitchen, every step reminding me of the severe pounding that Octavian had just given me. Maybe that was the reason why he had wanted me to do this chore.

I headed towards the fridge, opened it, and stuck my head inside. Suddenly, there was a blood-curdling scream behind me.

CHAPTER SIXTEEN

Excerpt from the journal of Jackson Jurgovan.

June 19, 2019- written later in the day

At the summer home of Octavian Segunda in St. Moritz.

I have to get my affairs in order now that I have proclaimed Octavian Segunda to be my True Master and he has accepted me as his Servant, at least for the time-being.

I need to call my father and tell him that I am moving to Switzerland. I don't think he will care as long as I keep sending him the checks that he has become used to receiving.

I need to call my financial guy and get him to transfer all of my assets to a bank here in Switzerland. Not that I will have need of anything as long as I am with Octavian, but I will feel better if my money is nearby.

I need to call the doctors and get my medical records and prescriptions transferred. I don't even know what the health care system here is like, but I'm sure it is first-class.

My house will need to be closed and the utilities will need to be stopped. My stuff will need to be packed and put into storage.

Cancel my cell phone plan.

I will have to ask Octavian about how to apply to the Swiss government for a VISA and which kind I will need.

The Service should be notified about what I have discovered about Octavian and know where I will be located from now on . . .

The scream came again from behind me — high-pitched and shrill.

I stood and turned around to see a man in a butler's outfit

standing across the kitchen. He was clutching his chest and continuing to scream.

"I am a guest of Octavian's," I said softly in way of explanation for why I was in the house. I hoped that he spoke English.

"He can't see you," Octavian's deep voice whispered behind me. "I've seen this face before many times." He pulled on the back of my robe until it came away from my body.

The butler turned slightly towards Octavian and screamed again. My new Master was completely naked and dripping water on the floor.

"He can see you," I whispered back at him.

"No fucking way," he said in disbelief. "Maro?"

The man dressed as a butler stopped screaming immediately and looked at Octavian strangely. "Herr Segunda?"

"Maro, it's me," Octavian said soothingly in German.

I could see the delight in Octavian's face as he looked at a man who normally would not be able to see him.

"Mr. Segunda, I'm so sorry. I came to clean today. I thought you were coming into town tonight."

"We got in late last night, Maro. I'm sorry, I should have told you."

He walked over to Octavian and touched him like he needed to verify that he was real. "It's so good to finally meet you, sir."

"Likewise." Octavian was still holding my robe in front of him and it just occurred to me that now I was completely invisible without it.

The butler looked nervously over to where I was standing. I quickly moved off to the side, but his eyes stayed steady on the spot that I had vacated. He really couldn't see me. I stuck my tongue out and made crazy eyes at him, but no response.

"I saw — I saw — the robe."

"I was holding the robe in front of me," Octavian said

quickly. He put the robe on now.

"No, it was—"

"Was what?"

"Full of someone. It was filled out."

"It was the light," Octavian lied to his butler. "The light only let you see the robe in front of me and not the rest of me."

The butler looked back and forth from the fridge to Octavian. He was trying to buy the story. "And did you open the fridge door?"

"Yes."

"I heard the robe say something."

"What did it say?"

"I'm not sure," he said slowly. His eyes were large and just a little crazed. "But I heard it."

"You heard me talking to myself as I came in from the hot tub."

"Maybe," he said as he looked back and forth again. "I'll just get out of your way then, sir." He looked at the refrigerator with uncertainty in his eyes.

"We won't need you until tomorrow, Maro. I'll make sure that I stay in one room while you clean the house."

"But I haven't cleaned yet."

"It's cleaner than any hotel I have ever stayed in, Maro. We'll be fine."

"We, sir?"

"Yes, Daniel, my driver and myself."

"Yes, sir. I'll be back tomorrow."

We both watched as Maro gathered his supplies and left the chalet. I turned to look at Octavian and he had a *what-the-fuck* look on his face.

"I'll translate what he said for you," he finally told me as he grabbed two waters from the fridge and handed me one.

"No need, Master. I understood him."

Octavian looked at me strangely. "You speak German?"

"No."

"Well, that's what he was speaking, Jackson."

"Really?"

Octavian reached up and scratched his head while he looked down at the water dripping off of him. "I drop a load deep in your ass and suddenly you are invisible and can understand German . . ."

"Can you wiggle your ears without touching them, Master?"

"No."

"Try." When I saw the withering look he gave me, I added, "Please, Master."

He easily wiggled them.

I giggled at him. "I give you a great fuck and suddenly you can be seen and can do what I can do . . ."

He growled and I stopped talking. "You will get punished for that, Servant, but I do like the way you think."

My cock started to harden at his promise of punishment, which gave me an idea. "Master, do you think that we switch abilities every time that I have your essence inside of me?"

"We didn't just switch abilities, because I can still speak and understand German."

"Oh, true. Okay, we are able to channel the other's abilities in addition to our own, then."

"Maybe. We will have to test it out tomorrow. But for today, I am going to fuck you over and over again until I get my fill."

"Yes, sir!" I watched as he grabbed two bottles of water from the open fridge.

"Back to the hot tub, invisible boy."

"Yes, Master." I wanted to go quickly, but the pain in my ass would not allow it, so I carefully hobbled my way back outside.

"I can see, despite your brilliance at taking me on my first try, that you are paying for that now, Servant."

"A necessary consequence for taking that big lap hog of yours, Master." I reached the hot tub and had to take a quick second to regather myself.

"So, you would do it again, Jackson?"

"I'm about to do it again in just a few seconds, Master."

"No regrets?"

"Not one," I said with a bravado I didn't quite feel as I walked up the stairs and very painfully swung my leg over the side of the tub. Before I succumbed to the pain, I quickly did the same to my other leg.

Octavian was right behind me and held me as I reached the middle of the hot tub. "I want you on my lap like we were before we were interrupted." He sat down at the back of the tub again.

I sat down on his lap facing him, feeling more intimate than ever.

He handed me a bottle of water and told me to drink. Octavian followed suit, draining his bottle.

I watched him carefully. He might have been the most handsome man I had ever seen, not because he had model looks or an athlete's body, but because he was exactly my type in every way.

"What does my new Servant have running through his pretty little head?" he asked with his deep rumbling voice that reminded me of thunder rolling down the valley of my hometown.

"I'm just very happy with you, Master."

"Glad to hear it. Now, let me show you just how happy your Master is with you." Octavian, with perfect timing, pushed his hard cock back onto my hole and inside me.

My eyes rolled into the back of my head as I bit down hard on my bottom lip. They say that the second time you do something that it becomes easier based on your knowledge that you have done it before. I wish the people that had said that could have just tried to take Octavian's monster once.

I wanted to give up. I didn't think I could take him this time. I arched my back, gripped his strong shoulders, my heart pounded in my chest, and sweat poured off of my brow as his cock continued to bully its way inside me once more. I was very young when I had realized that fucking felt different, depending upon the position, and that some angles worked better than others. It had not taken me long to figure out that a big cock goes inside easier in doggy-style than missionary. So, I knew this one was going to hurt a lot more than the last fuck.

"I can tell that it is not easy for you to take me, Jackson, but your ass also tells me something."

I opened my eyes and looked at him. There was no way I could have said anything.

"Your ass grinds back and down on my hammer like it can't get enough. You want all of me, don't you, Servant?"

I nodded. I hoped that my eyes didn't look glazed over, but the strain of him entering me was unlike anything I had ever experienced before. He seemed even bigger than the first time, which I didn't think was humanly possible, but here we were.

Finally, when I felt he was all the way inside me, I looked at Octavian and smiled. He put a hand on my chest and said, "Come on, baby. Open all the way up for me."

A shot of panic ran through me. *He wasn't all inside me?* I closed my eyes, arched my back, leaned back over his legs, and willed my ass to slide all the way down onto his fat cock. With great relief, I felt it happen and I settled onto his lap.

"Ahhhh. There it is," my new Master said to me.

I felt like the head of his cock was going to come up my throat, because he was so far inside me.

"You are a revelation for me, Jackson."

I didn't know what he meant, so I just looked at his beautiful face as I ground my ass back onto his flagpole.

"You wanted me to give you a hard fuck and then decide about our relationship for the future, did you not?"

"I did, Master."

"I have decided."

"I will accept your decision, no matter what, Master."

"You will do what I tell you to do," he growled.

I loved how absolute he was in his dominance of me. It made my balls tingle with excitement immediately. "Yes, Master."

"I have decided to treat you as a Servant in private and as my partner in public."

"Partner, Master?"

"My equal, Jackson. Now that you can be invisible like me, I feel like we can do great things together."

"I am honored, Master."

"You will be impaled on this big dick for many years to come, Jackson. It is me that is honored by you. We will have to experiment and see what the limits of your powers are."

His big cock holding open my anal ring was causing me not to be able to think very clearly. "I am not the one with the powers, Master."

"I think every NOMAR who was in my place with his dick up that fantastic ass of yours would disagree, Jackson."

Our subtle movements from just being on top of each other and feeling the blasts of water on my back, made me sweat as his steel pipe held me open. "I am just a tool for your pleasure, Master."

"Yes, you are. And a very tight tool, at that. Rarely has a man been able to remain so tight after I have fucked them. Yet another one of your special powers, Servant."

"I am unable to think of myself as special when I am mounted on you like this, Master. In fact, it is hard for me to think at all when you have me spread so wide open."

"Well, then, let me give you a good hard fuck so that you can clear your head."

"Yes, sir!"

Chapter Seventeen

Excerpt from the journal of Jackson Jurgovan.

June 19, 2019

At the summer home of Octavian Segunda in St. Moritz.

I need time to think.

Octavian has told me that he wants me to be his partner, but I'm not sure what that means.

I need time to process it.

He wants me to be his Servant in private!

I need time to celebrate.

Master says that he wants to use my invisibility to his advantage. I'm not sure what that means, either, but I would do anything for him.

I need time to negotiate with him.

He says he will keep me for a very long time. That he will have me mounted on his cock for years to come!

I need time to fantasize about that.

I haven't had a second to do any of these things. Mind you, I'm not complaining. Octavian has done nothing but shown me his total attention and kept me skewered on his big cock for the entire day, but I do need time to work through these details.

My new Master had carried me from the hot tub to his oversized bed while I was still mounted on his cock. He fucked me, doggy-style, one more time before finally withdrawing. It was an amazing show of strength and power. We slept, me as the little spoon, with his hot body wrapped around me. I went to sleep immediately, despite the pain of my ass.

"We have a lot to do today, Jackson."

I stirred at the sound of my Master's voice.

"I want us to experiment today," he continued.

I opened my eyes and he was above me, holding himself up with his massive biceps and forearms.

"I want us to see how far your new skills will take you, Jackson."

I considered myself fortunate that when I got up a few hours ago to take a piss that I decided to brush my teeth again. His face was very close to mine. "I am interested in that also, Master."

He smiled down at me. "Good. We are on the same page then, partner."

I reached down between our bodies and felt his rock-hard cock. I wrapped my hand around it, feeling the heat pouring off of it. "Seems we are also on the same page about something else, Master."

"Yes. The experiment definitely starts and ends with my cock planted once again inside that sweet ass of yours, Jackson."

I couldn't help but smile up at him. "We might have to experiment a lot then, Master, to make sure that we get it right."

He chuckled. "Worried that you are not going to get enough cock from me, Jackson?"

"You *are* a man with three Servants, Master."

"Something tells me that the others will have to defer to you."

"I better make the time I have you to myself matter then." I pulled my legs up and around him so that my thighs were flat on my chest. I hooked my arms under my knees and rested my feet on Octavian's hairy chest.

Octavian grabbed a bottle of lube from the nightstand,

straightened himself, and rubbed the slick liquid all over his massive cock. He tossed the bottle to the side of the bed and repositioned himself back over me.

We had not fucked in this position, since it was usually the hardest when a dick was as big as the one Octavian sported. I was a little scared of what was about to happen, but at the same time, thrilled that I was going to get to watch my new Master tear me up from above.

"I need to be inside you, Servant." Octavian's husky voice made my cock even harder.

"I need you inside me, Master."

"Same page . . ." He placed his cockhead against my ass-hole and pushed his hips forward.

I felt the heat pour off of his skin and heat my hole. He leaned down and placed his palms flat on my collarbone. He continued to work his hips forward, driving every bit of himself inside me. He didn't stop until there was none left to push inside. I was full of him again.

"You have an amazing ability to be tight as a virgin for me each time, Jackson."

The mental image of Rene's sloppy hole suddenly burst through into my consciousness. "I hope it continues, Master. Yours is by far the biggest cock I have ever had to bounce back from . . ."

"I have confidence that you will not disappoint me, Servant." Octavian began to slow-stroke his cock back and forth inside me.

I arched my back and my eyes fluttered as I got into his rhythm of fucking. I rode his long cock back and forth, loving the way that he kept me spread open the entire length of his dick.

Octavian was like a wave, completely enveloping and crashing on me. I had never felt anything like it. I wanted to drown in him. It was already hard to breathe, but I wanted nothing more than for him to smother me with his weight, his heat, and his hot cum. His cock was but a tool for the rest of this to happen to me.

My new Master fucked me like he had just released me from my cage on the first night of Servitude. His strokes were long and deep, each one seemingly more powerful than the last. The only thing that kept me from being banged against the headboard was Octavian's huge arms pushing down on my torso.

As he got faster, he lowered himself down until he was literally lying on top of me. The smell of fresh apples and cloves was overwhelming. It was everything that I could have wanted — like a bear rug covering my body and pushing me down into the mattress.

I kissed what part of his skin I could reach and licked the sweat off him. He tasted like pure man and I licked more, chasing that taste. My asshole was burning from the friction and from the stress of being stretched to its absolute limit, but I couldn't get enough of my new Master or his big dick.

Octavian leaned further down onto my chest and hooked his arms undermine. His head was to the side of mine and his lips were at my ear.

"I've never felt anything like when I'm inside you," he whispered as he continued to drive his cock deep inside my ass.

There was no way I could have spoken, so I made a humming noise to let him know that I was on the same page with him. I felt underwater by the man wave on top of me, but I couldn't have been happier about it.

My cock was so hard, his hot hairy body pressing down on it, doing nothing but stimulating it further. I was within seconds of coming without touching myself again.

I arched my back and hips, trying to press my throbbing cock to Octavian's hairy belly even more. As if he could read my mind, he pressed himself down on me until I erupted with my ejaculation. I sprayed my load between our sweaty bodies as my new Master continued to pump his manhood deep inside me over and over again.

"Oh, there it is," Octavian groaned. He redoubled his efforts.

I hadn't thought it possible for my new Master to fuck me any harder or deeper, but here he was proving me wrong. I licked my lips and tried to swallow.

"Give it to me, Master."

Octavian arched his back and roared with his release. He pumped me full of his life energy and warmed me from the inside out.

I wrapped my arms around his big chest and held onto his back as his cock continued to pump his hot seed inside me. I rode his thrusts until they subsided and he calmed.

"Let's see how long that lasts," he finally said.

I suddenly became awake. "You think I'm only invisible for a certain amount of time, Master?"

He looked at me with surprise. "I do."

"We will test it today?"

"Yes. Today. You will shower with me and we will go to town."

"How long do you think it will last, Master?"

"I'm not sure yet whether it is the amount of my cum inside you that matters or the time you have been carrying it."

"I'm not sure that I can stand to shower, Master," I said with a chuckle.

"I will carry you."

I felt safe in his arms, even in the shower. I busily scrubbed both Octavian and me clean, being careful not to blast my ass with the water. We wanted his load to stay inside me for our experiment.

We were soon dry, and Octavian was dressed in casual

khaki pants and a cream colored cable knit sweater. He completed the look with brown hiking boots that made me hard just looking at them. He looked good enough to eat on the spot.

"Bring a change of clothes," he commanded.

It was misting slightly as we left the chalet and headed towards Daniel's car, which was waiting for us on the street. Daniel must have seen us leave the house, because he exited the car and opened the back door for us.

I was having a hard time keeping my teeth from chattering. The wind was definitely whipping my naked body, even though Master was holding me to him. I watched Daniel's face carefully as we approached.

Daniel hesitated and made a move to close the car door, but stopped himself.

"It's okay, Daniel. It's me," Octavian said.

Daniel pulled a card out of his coat. *Master?*

I realized that the big bodyguard was getting his first look at Octavian after never having seen him for many years. I also saw that Octavian was not used to people looking at him and actually seeing him.

"It's me," Octavian reassured him. "This is what your Master looks like. Can you see Jackson?"

Daniel looked around and then shook his head.

Octavian pushed me inside the back of the car and said, "We are going into town, Daniel." He followed me inside.

On the back seat was a fur blanket. Octavian looked at me and said, "You're gonna need that to stay warm." He wrapped me in it and held me to his side. "It's your feet that are the worst, isn't it?"

I nodded to him knowingly, realized how stupid that was and answered, "Yes, Master."

Daniel was in the car and started it. We were soon on our way down the mountain.

"Stop at Hemminger's," Octavian told him.

Daniel soon pulled to the curb in front of a very expensive looking group of shops. I saw on the sign that Hemminger's was a jewelry store.

My Master squared himself to me and looked me in the eye. "I want you to steal something from the store for me, Jackson."

CHAPTER EIGHTEEN

Excerpt from the journal of Jackson Jurgovan.

June 20, 2019

At the summer home of Octavian Segunda in St. Moritz.

Sex with Octavian is beyond anything that I have even considered possible.

It is unbelievable.

I have never come without touching myself before, and now, almost every time Octavian fucks me, it happens.

I hope he never grows tired of me.

I hope he likes fucking me as much as I like him fucking me. He says he does, I think he does, but I want to be sure.

I will be anything for him. If he turns me permanently invisible by fucking me, then I will live my life with him as he lives it. I can't believe that I'm writing this, but it is true.

He says that we are leaving for Zurich today, which is fine, since I will let him fuck me on the private train car all the way back. But what will happen once we are back?

The thought of him with someone else makes my blood boil. Not because I am jealous. Well, I guess if I'm honest, it is because I am jealous, but of the time, not the person. I want to be with him every second of the day and night.

I wonder what my ass hole would look like after that?

I wonder what it looks like now . . .

I don't want to share him with his other Servants. Maybe he can pay them off early and send them home. Maybe I can . . .

Octavian and I were in the back of the car, and he had just

told me that he wanted me to steal something from the jewelry store for him.

I didn't want to question my Master, but I was not a thief. The last thing I wanted was to be arrested in a foreign country and be separated from him.

His face softened. "Don't worry, I will go back to the store and pay for whatever you take. I just want to see how stealthy you are. I will go with you to the store and will help distract the clerk."

"Yes, Master." I didn't feel bad about stealing, not if he was going to buy it anyway. He certainly could afford anything in the store, and hopefully buy my way out of jail if he needed to.

"Your footprints will give you away. Be careful to wipe your feet on the mat when you go inside. I will go inside first. You follow me."

I felt like there was a lot more advice he could have given me, but for whatever reason he chose not to say. Daniel opened the door and I slid out into the misty air. Octavian followed me, but once out of the car, did not even look my way. He headed towards the store.

I followed behind Master's long strides up to the door. It was opened by a doorman, who, I assumed, was also a security guard. The doorman greeted Octavian, but not me. Not knowing when the next customer might come, I slipped into the store behind Octavian. I carefully wiped my feet on the mat right inside the door, noticing that the floor was polished marble. Two feet inside the door, standing like silent guardians, were metal detectors. You had to pass through them to enter or exit.

Standing completely naked in a room full of people was a very weird experience, even though I was also completely invisible. The fact that I was a marked man doing so in a roomful of NOMARs made it even more strange. I looked around and saw that not one single person was looking at me. It made me feel very liberated. Instead, several salesmen were fawning over Octavian. He moved them off towards a case on the side of the room.

I headed for the opening of the main circle of jewelry cases. No one was there, but a manager type was at the back case. Looking down into the cases, I saw watches. I moved on. There were beautiful rings, bracelets, necklaces, and even cock rings.

My gaze was drawn to a spectacular platinum ring with a square cut emerald blazing on the top of it. It was my first choice, but I would have to wait. The cases were all locked and the keys were dangling from each salesperson's waist.

I moved to the next case and saw a fantastic diamond-encrusted tie clasp that I thought would look spectacular on my new Master. Moving to the next one, I didn't see anything that caught my eye, but in the last case in the circle was something that I couldn't pass up.

"Let me show you this over here," I heard the salesman say in German as he moved in my direction.

I easily understood him, even though I had never studied the language before. I pressed myself against the far case and waited for the man to come at me.

Master followed the salesman over, but stayed on the outside of the cases. He watched me with humorous eyes.

The salesman had stopped at the case with the tie pin in it and inserted his key into the lock. He slid back the case door while reaching inside. I stayed on the opposite side of the door, but I reached in as well. Being keenly aware that I couldn't move the tie clasp until after he looked away, I paused after I put my fingers on it.

The door was only partially pushed shut, so I was able to retract my hand after the salesman was showing Octavian some cuff links. I had the tie pin, but knew that anyone could see it floating in the air. I quickly put it on the counter in front of a sales sign. It could now only be seen by someone standing in front of the cases.

"I don't think I have need for those," Octavian said. He looked at me with a raised eyebrow and I pointed at the other two cases that I needed opened.

"I wouldn't mind seeing your cock rings," he said with a smirk in my direction.

I rolled my eyes and prepared for the door to be unlocked.

"What size, sir?"

"Oh, the largest they make, I believe."

I nodded my head for no one to see except my Master.

"Well, we only have a two-inch diameter here on display, but we certainly can tailor something to meet your needs."

"That's about ten inches too short for me, if you know what I mean."

The salesman looked so shocked by what Octavian was saying that he didn't notice the emerald ring floating out of the case and onto the counter in front of the sale sign. He held up the cock ring for my Master to look at.

"Yes, that definitely won't work for me." Octavian rounded the cases and looked into the last one I had indicated. "Maybe something like this."

The salesman looked through the glass to see that Master was pointing at what looked like a silver earring with the Swiss flag on top of it. He unlocked the case and asked, "Do you have a Prince Albert piercing?"

My hand darted like a cobra striking. I had what I wanted and I put it with my other trinkets.

"No, is that what that is?" Master played dumb. "I'm not sure I could ever pierce my cockhead." He looked at me questioningly.

I made the cut sign with my hand over my throat as I moved out of the circle of cases up to my stashed loot. Each one of the pieces had a complicated looking tag on them, so I carefully worked at getting each one off without anyone seeing me.

Master thankfully pulled the salesman away towards the back of the store. Once I had the tags off, I proceeded to wrap the three items in tissue paper that was stacked on the counter.

The next part of my plan had to happen fast. When no one was looking in my direction, I took what looked like a very expensive watch that was on display and I put it on the floor at my feet. I waited for the security guard to look to the side and I kicked the watch so that it slid through the metal detector and came to rest against the guard's boot.

Immediately an alarm sounded and the guards jumped into action. They came forward into the store.

With the guard gone, I threw the tissue ball high into the air and walked through the metal detectors. Catching the ball on the other side, I placed my package on the floor beside the door and turned around to look at my Master.

Octavian and the salesmen had moved to the front of the store with the alarm. Something was odd about him. My new Master was shimmering and part of him was already invisible.

It took me seconds to process what was happening. In one swift movement, I turned, picked up the tissue ball, hit the door to open it, and ran for the car. I became visible half-way across the sidewalk.

Fortunately for me, Daniel was at the car waiting with the door open. He smiled at me and produced a blank card which he quickly wrote upon and delivered to me once I was safe inside. *I see you now.*

The alarm was still going off when I jumped in the back seat and wrapped myself in the blanket. I didn't understand why Daniel was still holding the door open where the

spectators on the sidewalk could look inside and see me naked until I felt the seat depress beside me.

Octavian's deep voice said, "Thank you, Daniel." He was
completely invisible, but I knew he was naked beside, me so
my dick started to harden immediately.

Daniel shut the door and walked around to the driver's
side.

I watched Daniel's movement around the car, but my heart
was beating like it wanted out of my chest. I might have
looked calm, but I wasn't. "The police will be here shortly,
Master."

He had appeared enough for me to see half of his face now.
He smiled at me and said, "You were very clever in there,
Jackson. Show me what you got, Servant."

I opened the tissue ball and pulled out the emerald ring.
He took it and said, "Ah, yes. The most expensive thing in the
store. Is that your taste level, little one?"

I blushed furiously and said, "We can take it back, Master."

"Nonsense," he said, reaching for my hand. He slipped the
ring onto my finger and said, "It will have to be sized, of
course."

"Master is beyond generous. I'm afraid they will arrest me,
Master." I lowered my voice and whispered, "I was visible."

"They will not arrest you, Jackson."

"How can you be so confident, Master?" I asked as I heard
sirens approaching.

"Because I own the store, little one. Now, show me what
else you stole from me."

I smiled broadly at him and produced the diamond tie
clasp. "I thought you would look elegant wearing this, Master."

He took it from me and inspected it. "It is lovely. Thank
you, my Servant."

"And when I saw this, I knew I had to get it for you," I told him as I produced a glittering jeweled octopus broach from the tissue.

"Ohhhh. I love it! Thank you, Jackson," he said, right before planting his lips on mine and crushing me with them.

He took my breath away.

"Get dressed. Quickly, Jackson." The police cruisers pulled up right behind us.

I scrambled to put on my clothes and shoes in the back of the car.

"Listen carefully, Jackson. You are going to march into that store confidently and tell them who you are and that you belong to me. You are going to say that we were testing their security and it came up short. You will produce the three items for them to see, but you will not give them back to them. In fact, I don't want you to even take the ring off your finger."

"What if they do not believe me, Master?"

"Then tell them to call the corporate office and I will have the call routed to the car phone. By the way, afterwards, will you get my phone and wallet from the bathroom garbage can?"

I looked at him with an odd look on my face.

"When I saw you run, I knew what that meant, so I ran into the bathroom, stripped down, and followed you invisibly."

"Smart, Master." I slipped into my shoes, fully dressed now.

"It's not my first time being invisible, Servant. Now, go."

Daniel opened the door and I slid over Master's knees and out the door. Daniel closed the door behind me and I headed to the store. I saw two Swiss policemen stationed at the door. The alarm was still sounding.

As I approached the door, both policemen held up their hands for me to stop.

"I would like to see the manager," I demanded. My words came out in English.

"Not right now. The store has had a robbery." The policeman fortunately had excellent English.

"They are looking for this," I said as I produced my hand where I was wearing the emerald ring.

Both of the officers gaped at the ring on my finger before grabbing me by each arm and escorting me inside. The alarm stopped as we entered.

A policeman in a suit was speaking to the manager at the front set of cases. He turned and yelled something in German to the two policemen on either side of me. They answered him in German as we stood across the case from them.

"Are you the manager?" I asked the man speaking to the detective.

"I am."

"My name is Jackson Jurgovan. I am the Servant of Octavian Segunda."

"*The* Octavian Segunda?" the manager asked with awe in his voice.

"Yes."

"You have ID?" the detective asked.

I snapped at him, "Servants don't carry IDs."

"Convenient."

"We were just testing your security protocols, and needless to say, you failed miserably." I put my hand wearing the ring on top of the jewelry case for dramatic effect.

"Thief!" the manager yelled as he stared at the ring.

"Silence!" I said firmly back. I was amazed at how forceful and authoritative I sounded. I pulled the other two items out of my pockets and placed them on the counter. "You have a problem." I could tell from the look on the manager's face that he had not realized anything but the ring was missing.

"Why should we believe you?" the detective asked me in excellent English.

"You don't have to. Have him call the corporate office."

He turned to the manager, who removed a cell phone from his pocket and pecked at the screen, dialing a number.

"I will use your restroom while you are checking," I informed them.

"Go with him," the detective told the officers.

"Make him leave the ring," the manager said sullenly with the phone still to his ear.

"I will not."

The detective said, "He came in of his own volition. He will not do anything foolish."

"Of course not," I said firmly. "Why would I steal a ring when my Master can buy everything in this store twelve times over?"

No one bothered answering, so I made my way to the restroom and retrieved Master's clothes. I remembered that he just wanted me to grab his cell phone and wallet, but those boots that made me so hot were on top of his clothes and I definitely wanted to see him in those again. When I returned to the showroom, I heard Master's voice on the cellphone speaker. He was speaking in his most authoritative voice and in English.

"Be on notice that my Servant will be taking the three items with him when he leaves. You may charge them to my account. I will be hiring a team of security experts to prepare a plan for upgrades for the store in the next week."

"Yes, sir, Mr. Segunda, sir," the manager said nervously.

Chapter Nineteen

Excerpt from the journal of Jackson Jurgovan.

June 21, 2019

In the private train car of Octavian Segunda, bound for Zurich.

Octavian has determined that I have almost two hours of invisibility after he fucks me, which means that he can be seen by people for two hours. He seems thrilled by this prospect.

He has decided that we will keep the emerald ring, and the one of us who is visible will wear it. It will be a symbol of our partnership. I've always dreamed of finding a man like Octavian and now he was right in front of me. I'd better not screw this up.

My new Master gave me two hard fuckings after our outing to the jewelry store and dumped both loads deep into my ass. Four hours later, he made Daniel come and see if he could see me. He could, so we hypothesized that I had two hours of invisibility for each hot load that I carried inside me.

I'm excited to be travelling back to Zurich with Octavian, but I did like that he didn't have to work while we were away.

Master says that he has some work planned for us already. He has not elaborated, but my guess is that he is going to have to fuck me a few times before we start, so that is fine by me.

I'm curious to see what my new life holds for me. Will Master still be so attentive to me, with work and his other Servants so close? Will he really value me as a partner in his life like he said?

We shall see once we arrive in Zurich.

The train ride back home from the Alps was even more spectacular than the one that took me to St. Moritz. Of course,

I was fully impaled on Octavian's cock almost the entire trip. He fucked me in almost every position possible until I passed out from exhaustion.

I vaguely remember him carrying me out of the train station, which was pretty easy since I was invisible to everyone else but him. I woke up later that night with my stomach growling.

I tried to sit up and got a hot searing pain in my ass for my effort. I gingerly stood beside the bed and reached for the robe on the chair in the corner. Draping the robe around me, I walked to the bathroom and pissed before tying the sash.

My stomach was demanding food and I could smell it when I opened the door and stepped into the hallway. I was elated not to find myself in the Servants' suite of the mansion, but instead was one door down from Octavian's bedroom. I was also happy that I was not locked in my room or out of the dining room. Master had thought of everything.

I entered the dining room where I saw Octavian and his family already seated. "Good evening."

"Ah, Jackson," his uncle greeted me. "We were beginning to think you had been drugged or something."

"I'm sorry that I overslept," I quickly apologized.

"No need for that," his father told me. "Come and join us. Octavian was just telling us about your experiments in St. Moritz."

I looked down at my robe. "I'm afraid I'm not dressed or showered properly."

"Sit here, Servant," Octavian commanded. He was pointing at the rug by his chair.

I walked to the spot and tried to sit down on the floor without letting my ass be the first thing to hit the ground.

"Looks like you gave him the business on the way home, my nephew."

"He has an amazing ass, Uncle. It is hard for me to stay out of it."

Once I was settled on the rug, Octavian's over-sized hand was on my head and neck — rubbing and stimulating me. His touch made me hard as a rock.

"Oh, so he is a Servant now?" Julis asked.

I could not see their expressions from where I was.

Octavian answered, "He has chosen to be my Servant."

"He chose?" Nicolai asked to clarify.

My new Master looked down at me and asked, "Would you like to explain, Jackson?"

"We have some kind of weird connection, Octavian and I," I blurted out.

"I'm sure it has nothing to do with his money," Julis commented sarcastically.

I ignored the comment and continued, "When he fucked me for the first time, I knew what it was."

"Wait, you have already fucked him? Without any training?"

"Jackson is surprisingly gifted in that department."

Octavian's grandfather quipped, "So, he's a sloppy mess."

"Hardly. He's the tightest fuck I've ever experienced — each time."

"Good for you, Jackson," Julis said to me.

"He is my true Master."

"Your *what*?" Octavian's father asked me rather forcibly.

"Your son is my true Master."

"And you believe that, Octavian?"

"He is something that I have never experienced before, Father. I also felt something when I was inside him."

"That is lust, dear," his grandfather added.

"I definitely was lusting for him, Grandfather, but this was something else . . ."

"I am drawn to Octavian," I said from under the table.

"At one million dollars a year."

"I don't need the money."

Octavian was quick to jump back in. "He isn't asking for any money."

"Stand up, Jackson," Niccolai ordered.

I looked up at my Master, who nodded his head. I stood up with his help.

Niccolai was standing also. "You mean to tell me that you are going to be my son's Servant without a contract and without being paid for it?"

"Yes, sir."

"Why would you do that?"

"He is my true Master. I would do anything to be a part of his life, sir."

"I am going to make Jackson my partner in the business," Octavian said firmly.

The look on the faces of his relatives was like he had just slapped them across the face. There was silence at the table.

"Partner in the boardroom and a Servant in the sheets, so to speak," I said to lighten the mood.

"That will be enough, Jackson. Sit."

"Yes, Master."

"Octavian, you barely know this man."

"He can see me. He can see us. He is different."

"Is that enough?"

"He also becomes invisible."

"He what?" Julis asked.

"As far as we can tell, after a fucking, he can stay invisible up to two hours for each load of mine that he carries." Octavian rested his warm hand on the back of my neck and gently squeezed me.

"Although it is next to impossible to walk around without his huge loads sloshing out of me," I said from under the table.

Julis clapped his hands loudly and said, "This is

outstanding news, Octavian."

"It is?"

"Wonderful," his father echoed.

"I haven't even told you the best news yet," Octavian said, right before taking a large sip of his soup.

There was silence at the table and I imagined Master's relatives were pissed off at him for being so dramatic.

"Well?" his father finally asked.

I watched Octavian put his spoon down and wipe his mouth with his napkin before saying anything. He was certainly pausing for even more dramatic effect.

"When Jackson is invisible, I am visible."

"Visible?" both men asked in unison.

"Yes. Everyone can see me."

"How is this possible?" Niccolai's voice sounded distant, like he was asking his father the question. There was no reply that I heard.

Octavian answered, "I'm not sure. It is like we are connected in some way, Jackson and I."

"Connected, like being his true Master?"

"I guess, but I'm not sure. He seems to be able to channel me when he is invisible."

"Like what?"

"He can speak and understand German like I do."

"Outstanding," Julis said.

"He basically becomes you," Master's father said.

"In some ways, but he is still him and I am still me. I don't know how to describe it, but we are going to work on a project together this week as partners and at home he will be my Servant. This is the plan that we have agreed to and we will test it this week."

"And if it doesn't work out?"

Octavian looked down at me and answered, "Then he will have to be happy having me fucking him on a regular basis here after I come home from work each day." He dipped a large roll into his soup and handed it down to me.

"You will keep him anyway?"

"We are connected and that is that."

It warmed my heart and made blood rush to my cock that Octavian was dedicated to being with me regardless of how our partnership worked out. I loved that he was so decisive with his answer, but I worried that if I did not perform this week whether that would have an effect on our relationship or not.

CHAPTER TWENTY

Excerpt from the journal of Jackson Jurgovan.

June 22, 2019
In the home of Octavian Segunda.

Strange occurrences since I got to Switzerland –
Saw a naked man emerge from an office building and he was one of the hottest men I had ever seen.
Discovered that he was invisible.
Found out that I could see him if we both were hard at the time. This wasn't hard for me, because the man was smoking hot as hell.
The man turned out to be Octavian Segunda, a billionaire recluse in Zurich.
He would only allow me to blow him, which I found to be truly desirable, but I wanted more.
Met the rest of the invisible family.
Octavian took me to St. Moritz on his private train car.
In the hot tub, we fucked for the first time. It was magical and I realized immediately that Octavian is my true Master. There is no doubt in my mind, but he seems hesitant.
We discovered, thanks to the housekeeper, that after Octavian fucks me that he becomes visible and I become invisible, at least for a period of time.
That period of time appeared to be about two hours for each load of Octavian's spunk that is inside me.
I agreed to be Octavian's Servant. He wanted me to be his partner in public and his Servant at home.
I find that while invisible, I gained other talents, like being able

to speak and understand any language in which Octavian is fluent
  I robbed a jewelry store at his behest.
  The store turned out to be owned by Octavian, so I didn't get into any trouble. He makes me go back inside after I'm visible and rub it in their faces.

"May I just move into your bedroom, Master?" We had been back for more than a week and so far, Octavian had not been able to make it through a single day or night without fucking me.

"I thought you wanted me to treat you like a Servant in our private lives, Jackson."

"I do, but I was just trying to make it easier for you, my Master." I was currently sitting on top of him, holding onto the headboard of his bed while his still-hard cock pushed more of his life-force inside me. My dick was still hard, bouncing on his belly, so I could see my invisible Master with no problem. Not that I needed it, because I could always see him when I was impaled on that cock of his.

"I've already made it easier on myself by having your bedroom be next to mine, Servant. If I wanted, I could have you staying upstairs with Joaquim."

Thank God he didn't do that . . .

"I am fortunate, Master." We had already said goodbye to Octavian's older Servant, Rene, earlier in the week.

"You are insatiable. That's what you are, and I am the fortunate one to get to try to satiate you on a daily basis."

"Oh, I am the one who is insatiable?" I asked in a sarcastic tone.

"Careful," he warned with a wag of his finger.

"My apologies, Master."

"I want you to go get clean and meet me in the study. I have plans for us this weekend and I want to go over them with you."

"Do those plans involve me doing this, Master?" I thrust

my hips up and back down again hard into his crotch. The feeling of his big fat cock spreading me wide open was euphoric.

"I don't think that will be necessary, Servant."

"It always seems necessary to me, Master."

"You will do as I direct you to or you will be punished." His tone was stern, but I knew he was kidding.

"Mmmmm . . . what kind of punishment, Master?"

"The kind where you won't be allowed to do that for quite a while."

"Message received, Master."

He popped me hard on my ass cheek and said, "Good. Now, go get pretty. I'm excited to tell you about our plans."

I wondered about those plans the whole time that I was in the bathroom. By the time I had showered, shaved, and groomed myself, I had run through a whole gauntlet of possible scenarios. I hoped it did not involve me having to do any more shoplifting, because I was not made for it.

Finally coming back into the bedroom, I saw that Octavian was gone. I got dressed in a t-shirt, shorts, and slides before following after him. It took me a few seconds to find the study, but I eventually opened the right door.

Octavian was seated behind his desk and was talking on the phone. I didn't want to bother him, so I quietly closed the door behind me and went to look at the octopi in their tanks. I especially liked the blue and gold one, and he seemed to like me. He put on a show for me of swimming and then suckering himself to the front glass of the cage.

"He is a flirt." Octavian's deep voice ran right through me to my soft parts like a knife through hot butter.

"Takes one to know one."

"I guess," he admitted with a chuckle. "His name is Sabi."

"He is beautiful."

He touched the side of my face with his open hand and

turned me towards him. "Not as beautiful as you are when no one but me can see you."

"Master . . ."

"We have many plans to discuss, Jackson. Let's get started. Please sit." He indicated a chair in front of his desk. Octavian sat and steepled his thick fingers in front of his face.

I sat down wondering if we were partners now and not Master and Servant.

There was a dramatic silence between the two of us.

"This is more complicated than I assumed it would be," he finally said.

"Why is that?" I purposely left off his title of respect to test to see if he considered us partners or not.

He chuckled. "I would like you mounted on my cock while I tell you this. It is hard to see you as a partner when I am in love with your ass so much."

"That can be easily rectified." I was thrilled that he was trying to keep this part of our relationship professional, but I also wanted to be mounted on his big rhino horn.

He raised an eyebrow and asked, "Easily?"

I blushed immediately and corrected myself, "Well, not so easily on that big stick of yours, but we can make it happen."

"No. I want to try to stay professional, if possible."

"Very well. I will just have to up my game when next I am your Servant."

"And when next I am your Master."

"Indeed."

Octavian shuffled some papers on his desk and then looked back up and into my eyes. "This weekend, Switzerland is hosting a summit. A secret summit."

I assumed since I was his partner and not his Servant, that I could ask questions and freely give my opinions. "What kind of summit?"

"Military in nature. The Chinese and the Americans are

discussing what to do about Iran, but I am mainly interested in the arms deals that will take place."

I thought for a moment. "You have an investment in an arms company?"

"Yes. Several."

"And how do you know of this summit if it is secret?"

"I've been asked to be on the Swiss delegation. We are tasked with trying to regulate the information surrounding weapons of war. Ultimately, we would want to keep the lines of communication open and the information flowing so that countries do not develop more hostility towards each other than they already have. And of course, I want to know everything. I don't like being surprised."

I was shocked by this news. I just assumed that everyone knew Octavian was a recluse to hide the fact that he was invisible. "You're gonna be on the delegation?"

"I'm afraid I have no choice. Of course I turned them down. But they countered with the fact that I would be able to Skype my appearance instead of actually being there."

"But that doesn't work either, Master."

He lowered his head and grinned at me. "I am not your Master in this instance, Jackson."

"Sorry, habit."

"I know. I will Skype the meeting and have the camera pointed at something else, of course. Maybe Sabi will make a good replacement for me. I feel as if I am unable to get out of this. The Federal Council called, and the President, personally asking me to be a member of the delegation."

"Wow. You are soooo powerful," I teased.

He narrowed his eyes and growled. "Don't think that I can't become your Master instead of your partner in a heartbeat. I will turn you over my knee right here and spank you, if necessary."

I slowly swallowed, trying to figure out what to say to him.

He made me a lump of silly putty with just a few words. I had never been unsure of myself before and no man had ever had that effect on me.

Octavian stood from behind his desk and walked around to the front. He leaned against his desk and surprisingly, it didn't move. He put two fingers under my chin and lifted my eyes to his. "I love that you challenge me, Jackson, but I will not let you forget that I am your Master."

I swallowed hard again. "Of course, Master."

He let go of my chin, but his gaze continued to penetrate into my soul. "I will need you to be inside of the American delegation. They will have the most information and influence."

"You want me to be invisible and find out what I can from their meeting?"

"I am more interested in what they say before, between, or after the meetings. I will be able to hear what they say at the meetings, so when they meet, you can take a break until they come back."

"I understand, sir."

"You will camp out in the American delegation room. You, as an American, will understand the subtle nuances of the way they will say in private to each other. You will have to eat while you are there and make sure you are not seen at all times, do you understand?"

"Yes, sir, but won't this just give us one side of the story? I mean we should know what the Chinese are thinking and planning also, right?"

"Unfortunately, neither of us speak Mandarin. I do have my man on the inside of the Chinese delegation, but he has proven to be . . . unreliable in the past. I'm hoping that we can get the full story with the two parts we will have."

"I see."

"This week we will practice and work on memory

techniques. I want you to be able to recall a large amount of information precisely to me at the end of each day."

"Yes, sir." This sounded daunting to me.

"Don't worry, little one. You will be mounted on my stiff prick while we practice. You will enjoy every minute of it."

I slightly bowed my head. "As I do every minute with you, Master."

He chuckled and said, "Oh, look who is so obedient to me now."

I blushed and said, "I try, Master."

He cupped the side of my face in one large hand and agreed with me. It was a tender moment that made me like him even more than I already did. He playfully smacked me on the cheek and returned behind his desk.

"I have some more papers to go through, but I want you mounted on my pike within the hour, Jackson. Go enjoy yourself until then."

"I'm sure I will enjoy myself even more when the hour is up, Master."

He looked up at me and said, "I have never met a man who could take my big cock and so look forward to the next time that he had all of me inside him again like you."

"I'm a true cock hound, Master."

He made a humming sound of satisfaction. "Cock bound might be more like it this time . . ."

CHAPTER TWENTY-ONE

Excerpt from the journal of Jackson Jurgovan.

June 23, 2019

In the home of Octavian Segunda.

Octavian wants me to spy for him.

There was a secret arms meeting that was going to be held in Zurich between the Americans and the Chinese.

Octavian was going to be in on the meetings, but he wanted me to be in the room with the Americans to hear what they say before and after.

I hadn't been worried about any part of it, except what he would have demanded after the meetings were over each night. He has already told me that he expects total recall of what was said, exactly as it was said. I've always been a big picture person, so I'm most worried about this.

Octavian told me that he was going to help me practice at remembering things . . . to improve my memory. We starting working on that right away.

The first thing Master did was sit me down in his lap — his thick pole stretching my ass hole wide. He gave me a list of twenty-one words to memorize. It was very distracting to have his hot cock throbbing inside me while I was trying to concentrate, but I did my best.

He took the list away from me and asked me for the words. With each correct response, he pulled my ass up and slammed it back down on his big dick. I didn't do so well.

Next, he gave me a grid of twenty-four pictures. Each picture was of some type of household item. He gave me five minutes to study it, but during the whole time, he fucked my ass like he'd just been re-leased from prison. It was one of the most powerful and complete fucks I had ever experienced and we both came at the end of the five minutes. Needless to say, I couldn't remember shit from those pic-tures . . .

"I want you to imagine a mansion, Jackson," Octavian told me.

I was on all fours, once again speared by his tremendous harpoon, so a mansion was not in my mind at all. My nose, however, was full of his smell — masculine musk, fresh ap-ples, and cloves.

"Yes, Master."

"How many rooms are there?" He continued to pull his thick cock out of my backside and pull my hips back towards him to once again sink deep inside my bowels.

I moaned, "Infinite, Master."

"Excellent. How many floors are there?" He pulled almost all the way out of me before slamming himself back inside me as deep as he possibly could.

"Many, Master. I have never explored them all to see."

"Good. Now I want you to imagine that you are on the first floor at the first room. Can you see it from the doorway?" This time he double pumped me.

I closed my eyes to concentrate and swallowed several times before I could find my voice. "Yes, Master. It has a sign on the door with a large number one painted on it."

"Excellent. Go to the room and open the door."

He was silent and still for a few seconds.

"What do you see in the room, Jackson?" This time, my Master hunched into me quickly and often.

"I see us fucking on the bed, Master."

"What position?"

"The one we are in now, Master."

"Very well. Remember what the room and the bed look

like, Jackson. Do you have it?" He gave me three quick thrusts to accentuate his point.

"Yes, Master."

"Good. Now, we are going to turn completely around and open the door right behind us. It should be labeled number two. Do that now, Jackson."

In my mind, I created the scene he was crafting.

"Open the door, my Servant."

I did while I felt him slow-fuck my ass.

"What do you see in the room?"

"I see us fucking, Master."

I heard his sharp intake of breath as he settled against my backside. "Are we going to be fucking in every room of your mansion, Servant?"

"God, I hope so, Master."

"Still not getting enough of me, Servant?"

"If there was just a way you could always be inside me, Master . . ."

He laughed. "Wouldn't that be something. And what position are we in now, Jackson?"

"I'm up against the wall, Master, and you are fucking pounding my ass into it."

Octavian thrust into me several more times. "Hmmm. I like this room."

I moaned shamelessly.

"Keep going," he commanded gruffly as he continued to pound his fat stick inside of me.

"Door number three. Me in a sling. Door number four. You on your back. Door number five. Us in the tub. Door number six. Me bent in half between the bathroom sinks. Door number seven. Missionary. Door number eight. Me on my knees blowing you. Door number nine. Me bent over the ottoman. Door number ten. You holding me upside-down."

"That's quite enough, Jackson," Master told me with a

laugh.

"I can keep going, Master."

"I'm counting on it, Servant." Octavian reached over and handed me the sheet of twenty-four pictures from my last memory challenge. "Put each object in one of the rooms, Jackson. Do it now."

The first picture was of a daisy in a vase. "We are on the bed. I am being fucked on all-fours by you, Master. The flower is on the nightstand beside the bed."

Octavian started to plow my ass with earnest. "Next," he ordered.

The next picture was of a dinner plate. I tried to speak, but found myself to be a bit breathless from the fucking was I being given. I gathered myself and tried again. "It is on a hotel tray with other empty dishes on the floor beside the bed while you fuck me against that wall, Master."

"Very good. Keep going."

I placed all of the objects into the rooms on that floor of my mansion. It took a while and some effort, but afterwards, Master pushed me flat to the mattress and poured his hot seed inside me. It was a whole new experience to be bred by this man who knew how to make my body open to all of the pleasures imaginable.

Later, in the shower, I absentmindedly scrubbed Master's back with a loofah. "Master, have you spent any time with your other Servant?"

"Why would you ask me that, Jackson?"

"I just don't want to be the jerk who takes all of your attention away from Joaquim, Master."

"Had enough of me?"

"Never, Master." I had to admit that my ass was burning and felt like it was on fire after Octavian fucked me, but there was no way I was ever going to deny him. "I just know how I would feel if my Master never visited me."

He put one large palm on my right cheek. "You are sweet. I will make time for him after the conference. We have too much training to get through this week."

"More training? How did I get to be the luckiest marked man alive?" I continued to scrub my big man's broad back.

"You could see the invisible man and then you had the nerve to turn invisible yourself."

"All prompted by my lust for you, Master."

Octavian laughed as he turned around and held me in his arms. "I am the one that can't seem to get enough of you, Servant."

"We are a pair, Master. I think we were made for each other."

"My dick was certainly made for being inside your ass," Octavian said with a growl as he reached around me and grabbed my ass.

"My body comes alive when you are on top of me, Master."

Octavian let go of my ass and looked at me with serious eyes. "Do you think you're going to be able to pull this off, Jackson? The stakes are very high."

"I will try my best, Master." I wasn't sure that I actually could pull it off, but I didn't want to admit that to him and risk him losing interest in me.

"You better."

I reached down and grabbed the thick cock swinging between his legs. I lovingly stroked it with my soapy hands. "I look forward to Master's constant attention for the rest of my training."

"Your attention to detail will be what makes you successful, Jackson. If you put your focus on being totally unseen when invisible, you will make the perfect spy."

"It will be a challenge for me, Master."

"You are totally focused on me when we are fucking, Jackson. Take that same attention to the assignment."

"I will try, Master."
"You will do it. Say it."
"I will do it, Master. It will be done, Master."
"It better be, Servant."

CHAPTER TWENTY-TWO

Excerpt from the journal of Jackson Jurgovan.

June 25, 2019
In the home of Octavian Segunda.
Octavian wants me to spy for him.
I don't mind being a spy, but I don't think that I will be a very good one. I am too hyper and don't pay attention to details as well as I could in a room full of men. They are my distractions and I know it better than anyone.

The pressure to be able to remember everything said and then repeat it to Octavian is very high. He has explained to me that even one word of difference between what was said and how I remember it, could be disastrous. I do not want to disappoint him or be the reason for him making a terrible business decision.

We have practiced for days now. My memory has increased an impressive amount under Octavian's tutelage. His unusual teaching methods where he fucks me hard to try to take my focus away from the task and then rewards me by fucking me more when I give the right answer has done wonders for my ability to retain information.

I was sad to see his training come to an end.

The conference is this morning, so I need to get going. Daniel will be waiting on me.

Daniel stopped the car in front of the main building at the University of Switzerland. I looked out of the window in awe of the rounded front of the building. It was impressive and not a government building, so the secret assembly would remain so.

Octavian and I had gone over the building schematics, so now I felt confident about where I was supposed to go. Daniel held a card up from the front seat.

Good luck, Jackson

"Thank you, Daniel. I'm just hoping that I will be able to walk after the fuckings Octavian just gave me."

I was completely naked in the back seat of the car. Octavian had fucked me four times, dropping his loads deep inside me each time. He had placed a butt plug inside me to keep all of his jizz from pouring out as I walked. The butt plug was made of a clear jelly-like substance that was invisible when I was invisible. I would be invisible for at least eight hours.

Daniel opened the car door for me and I exited in a hurry. I didn't want anyone to notice that no one got out of the car, so I pushed the door closed behind me quickly. Daniel was surprised, but covered it well.

I took off for the large university building in front of me. People were constantly moving into and out of it. I snuck through the revolving door behind a thin man in a suit.

Stopping inside the door, I made sure I wiped my feet on the doormat thoroughly like Octavian had taught me. The marble floors would show my footprints, so I could not linger long anywhere. I headed for the conference rooms on the third floor.

Octavian had explained to me that each contingent would have their own conference rooms at the opposite ends of the floor and that the large room in the middle would be the negotiations room.

There were no signs or designations on the doors, but I could tell from the security guys surrounding the ends of the hallway which room was which. I headed towards the Americans and slipped into the room behind a security guard of some sort. The door closed behind us as if by itself and he began sweeping the room for bugs. There were several other men in the room that seemed to be doing the same thing.

I was happy to see that there was thick carpet on the floor, but unfortunately, the pile was so thick that it also would show the depressions of my feet. I knew that I had to find a recess or corner to stand in so that no one would notice that. A quick look around the room rewarded me with the perfect spot to stand in.

From a recessed alcove in the middle of the room, I watched as the security guys slowly left the room. I was alone for maybe five minutes until the door opened and an explosion of noise entered.

A contingent of twenty men entered and they were all in loud conversations with each other at once. I recognized one of the men immediately. It helped that he was the tallest, broadest and most handsome amongst them.

I only knew him as the Duke. We had met at an orgy arranged by my former Master, Sully. The Duke had fucked me during the orgy and then asked my Master if he could come back two more times. I only knew him as a former Navy SEAL turned military contractor. He oozed masculinity and my dick got hard just looking at him.

I immediately wondered if Octavian knew about the Duke and my connection to him. Surely, he would have thoroughly investigated the men on each side of the table. Maybe the Duke's connection to the mob was not well documented. I decided Octavian did not know or he would have warned me.

The Duke sat down at the table towards the front and placed a laptop down in front of him. I suspected that he was probably more important to this contingent than I'd first thought. He was dressed professionally, with a black blazer over a black t-shirt that hid his muscular chest and arms.

The other men quickly took seats at the table. Most of them looked like pencil-pushers dressed in typical suits and ties. One suit was definitely in charge—he sat at the head of the table, but his body language showed disinterest.

The discussion started and the Duke quickly presented an opinion. They were arguing about what type of strategy to use with the Chinese. He pressured the others to consider his point of view. He was confident and aggressive, two qualities that I really liked in a man.

I listened carefully and used Octavian's memory techniques to commit the argument to memory. Each point, I placed into a room in my mansion. I didn't know many of the speakers' names, but I placed each one into the room with me and gave each a nickname based on his looks.

The Duke was starting to win the argument. I could tell that his points were starting to hit home with most of the men. The tension was building until the guy in charge called for a vote. The vote went the Duke's way.

"Booya!" The Duke was all smiles as he fist-pumped the air and closed his laptop.

"Hah!" I said, without thinking about it.

I quickly covered my mouth with my hands. I couldn't believe that I had made a sound, but the Duke's pet phrase that I had completely forgotten about had surprised me. I had heard the *booya* before, each time that he had fucked me right after he dropped his load deep in my guts. I had thought it was ridiculous then and especially now.

My heart dropped into my stomach when I saw the Duke's head turn in my direction. He had heard me, but now he was questioning who had made the sound. I would have to move from my location as soon as everyone went back to talking. I stood perfectly still and silent after that.

A lot of the men got up from the table and went to the sideboard, which was loaded with coffee, juice, pastries, and cereals. The Duke and the leader exchanged some words, which I couldn't hear, so I moved closer to them.

The leader was talking about who was going to present

what material to the Chinese. He was making the agenda. The Duke seemed to be listening, but then I saw him turn his head towards me.

Impossible, I thought. I had not made a sound, except for my earlier outburst. I watched in wonder as the Duke lifted his head and breathed in deeply through his nose. He was smelling me.

I had been careful not to use any deodorant, soap, nor shampoo that had any scent to it. Octavian had been adamant about that. *Was he smelling my sweat?* I was nervous, but didn't think I was sweating that much.

The sound of a chime melodically reverberated in the room. Most of the men stood and started to file out of the door. The Duke stayed behind for a minute.

"Jonah, can you look something up for me?" he asked one of the younger suits.

"Sure, Mr. Franks."

"I'm curious about where someone is. A marked man named Jackson Jurgovan."

My heart skipped a beat. I froze in place, in disbelief that he would have remembered my name.

"An American?" Jonah asked.

"Yes, and marked."

"That should make it easier. I'll have an answer for you when you return."

The Duke looked my way again and said, "Thank you." He left the room in a hurry.

I was left in the room with four men who were suddenly very busy laughing and eating.

Going back to my alcove, I gingerly took a seat inside it. I had to slouch as I sat down because I didn't want to sit on the butt plug and make my ass even more uncomfortable.

I wanted to close my eyes and review my memory mansion to make sure that I remembered everything correctly. I couldn't keep my eyes closed for too long, because I was nervous that one of the men left in the room would trip over me.

The American contingent was gone for more than two hours. I was bored as fuck by the time the door opened and they poured back inside. I stood and perked up.

The Duke immediately pulled Jonah over to the side of the room, close to where my alcove was located. "What did you find out?"

"Sir?"

"About the marked man, Jonah?" The Duke sounded impatient.

"He is here, Mr. Franks."

"Here?" The Duke nervously looked over his shoulder.

"Here in Zurich, sir. Didn't you know?"

"No, I didn't."

"He was travelling through Europe, but a man named Octavian Segunda has recently applied for a VISA for him. I assume he is currently living with the man since the application lists that as his home address. Do you know him, sir?"

"We all know him, Jonah."

"Sir?"

"He is a member of the Swiss delegation."

"Really? Do you think this Jackson is in the building, sir?"

"No. His Master is not, so I doubt he would be."

"I thought you said Mr. Segunda was a part of the Swiss delegation?"

"I did, but he is not in the building. He is Skyping from his office or his house."

"Oh, is he the octopus?"

"Excuse me?" The Duke sounded distracted.

"One of the guys was telling me that there was a monitor with a blue octopus on the screen."

"Yeah, that's him."

"Weird."

"He is one of the richest men in the world, Jonah. If he doesn't want to be on the screen, I'm pretty sure that no one is going to say a word about it. He could give two shits what you think is weird."

"Sorry, sir."

"Jonah, find out where he lives for me, won't you? And I'm going to need a phone number."

"Yes, sir."

The Duke took his seat at the table and the rest of the men followed suit.

CHAPTER TWENTY-THREE

Excerpt from the journal of Jackson Jurgovan.

June 26, 2019

In the home of Octavian Segunda.

The first day of the secret meeting was much more exciting than the second one. The first day re-introduced me to the Duke. He had actually said my name and asked for my current location.

Yesterday had involved a morning session, lunch, and an afternoon session, but today was just a morning meeting.

I had gotten through all three meetings and successfully reported back to my new Master with the details. Octavian had been very happy to hear the information that I had relayed to him. We had outdone ourselves with our fucking afterwards.

One thing that Octavian had not liked to hear was that I had made a noise while trying to remain unseen. He told me a story about how the same thing had happened to him several times, so he understood, but still didn't like it.

My new Master was also very curious about the Duke being able to smell me. He sniffed me all over and said that he did not smell anything that should have drawn his attention.

There was no afternoon session today, so I'm curious what Octavian has planned for us during this free time. I'm excited to find out.

Octavian and I were at lunch with his father and grandfather when Konju stepped into the room full of invisible men and me.

"Sorry to interrupt, Mr. Segunda, but there is a visitor at the front door to see you."

"You know what to do, Konju," Octavian said flatly.

I assumed that he never saw visitors.

"Yes, of course, sir. The normal protocols are in place, but this visitor is a man from the current project you are working on."

"From the summit?" Konju had my Master's full attention now. He looked at me.

"The Duke," we both said in unison.

"I assumed this would happen," Octavian said placing his silverware down on his plate. "I just didn't assume that it would happen so quickly. Konju, settle him in the study and I will be there shortly."

"Yes, sir." The steward left the room.

"You are going to see this man?" Octavian's father asked in disbelief.

"Yes. He is actually here to see Jackson, I believe."

Both of the older men turned to look at me.

I shrugged my shoulders. "A former fuck."

"You must be some fuck," Nicolai commented.

"You have no idea," Octavian told him. "I will put on bandages and see what he wants."

"You know what he wants," his grandfather said, using his spoon to point at me. "He wants to dip his wick in your Servant again."

"I'm sure he does," Octavian said as he stood up and headed for the door. "But, he will pay for that privilege with more than just his prick. Jackson, I will call for you in a few minutes. Be ready."

"Yes, Master." Octavian did not hear my acceptance, because he had already left the room.

"How does he even know that you are in Switzerland?" Julis asked me.

"He kinda heard me the other day at the meeting and then he smelled me."

"Two common hazards to being invisible," Octavian's grandfather admitted with a shrug.

"But he knew you were there?"

"No, I think he just thought of me or something. He didn't know I was there, but was reminded of me in some way."

Julis said, "That is a good outcome. Not bad for your first trip out, Jackson."

"Second—I robbed a jewelry store on my first trip out as an invisible man," I said with a large smile and a wink.

"Naughty," Octavian's grandfather said, while continuing to eat.

Ten minutes later, Konju appeared in the dining room to tell me that Octavian was requesting my presence in the office.

I was wearing sweats, but I removed everything but my jock strap before entering Octavian's office. I could see the back of the Duke's head as he sat in a chair facing the desk. A sudden pang of remorse hit me when I saw my beautiful Master sitting behind the desk completely wrapped in bandages. My heart went out to him.

I walked over to a spot between them and dropped down into The Service Squat.

The Squat was painful, but I fell into it without thinking. My legs spread, my head bowed, my forearms resting on the tops of my thighs, and all done while balancing on the tips of my toes.

"Master," I said without any emotion in my voice at all.

"Jackson, you remember the Duke, don't you? He has come to visit you."

"Good afternoon, sir," I said, without picking up my head or falling out of the Squat.

"You have humbled him. It is his fire that I remember."

"Jackson still has that fire when he is my partner, but right now he is my Servant and he knows that . . . fire is not allowed."

"You have him as your partner and your Servant?"

"Indeed I do."

"That is odd, isn't it?"

"It is unusual, but it is working out very nicely for us."

"I would think it would be more problem than solution."

"Jackson, you may speak freely," Octavian commanded. "And please stand and face us."

I slowly stood, looked at The Duke, and asked, "So Duke, are you here to discuss the conference or are you missing the feeling of your big dick being buried up to the nuts in my tight ass?"

"There's the fire."

"The latter, I would guess," Octavian said slyly.

The Duke turned to Octavian and said, "I certainly would enjoy a moment to . . . reconnect with Jackson, Mr. Segunda. And of course, I would love to see how you have mastered him, as well."

"And what do I get from this . . . reconnection?"

The Duke looked over at me and licked his bottom lip. "What would you like?"

"Information."

The Duke looked at me hungrily as he said, "That can be arranged."

"Just like that? Is his ass that good?"

The Duke quickly turned back to look at Octavian. "Haven't you had it?"

Octavian laughed. "I certainly have, many times."

"He is a treasure."

It was now Octavian's turn to look at me. "That he is."

"I would have had him as my Servant if I would have known that he was available."

"I guess I was lucky to have found him first."

"I will not compromise our mission, but I will consider any

questions that you might have and answer the ones that I can."

"Deal." Octavian held out a gloved hand to the Duke.

The Duke shook his hand.

"How about tomorrow night? You can come for dinner and spend the night with us. You can leave for the meetings the next morning after breakfast."

"Excellent." The Duke stood and shook both of our hands, which I found to be quite odd.

Konju was waiting at the door to escort the American out of the house. He looked super annoyed.

Octavian immediately took his gloves off and his bandages. He looked totally relieved to be free of them.

"Are you disappointed in me, Master?"

"No. Why would you ask that?"

"I have drawn undue attention to you and us."

"Yet it has worked out in our favor, no?"

"Yes, it has." I felt so relieved that Octavian was not angry with me.

"We have to be very careful around him in the future, little one."

"He is harmless, Master," I said with confidence.

My Master sat back down and opened a wooden box sitting on top of his desk. "I don't trust him and I suspect that he has a larger role in this summit than anyone knows."

I was impressed with his ability to read the man in such a short amount of time. "Yes, Master. Do you think he could hurt what you are trying to do?"

Octavian rolled a cigar between his thick fingers before answering. "No. I will get the information that I need, but I do not want any surprises out of him."

I loved his confidence and his control. "Do I surprise you, Master?"

He lit his cigar and spoke without removing the tip from

between his teeth. "If you are able to walk tomorrow after I finish with you tonight, you certainly will, Servant."

I was left speechless.

"Close your mouth and get your ass to my bedroom, Servant."

CHAPTER TWENTY-FOUR

Excerpt from the journal of Jackson Jurgovan.

June 27, 2019

In the home of Octavian Segunda.

Octavian seems pleased with my reports from the summit, so far. I am still fearful that I am going to screw this up somehow for him.

The Duke came to visit yesterday. He wants to fuck me again and told my new Master that he would have called for me to be his Servant if he would have known that I was available. Normally, this news would have elated me beyond belief since the Duke was the best fuck that I had ever had, but now I have found even better, so there is no contest.

He and Octavian agreed on a deal—information for my ass. Octavian didn't ask my thoughts on the matter, but somehow, I believed he knew them anyway. I certainly won't mind another fuck session with the Duke and if it benefits my new Master in some way, all the better.

I will try my best to get anything out of him that I can when we are together. Any little thing might be helpful to Octavian, so I will keep the Duke talking at the very least.

The worst part of the whole ordeal is that my Master will not be able to fuck me today, or I will be invisible to the Duke. Octavian will have to go to dinner in bandages.

It's time for dinner, so it's showtime for me . . .

Dinner with the Duke and my Master was uncomfortable. Both men were enamored with my ass and wanted nothing more than to rip my clothes off and fuck me blind on the table top, but I would have never known it. They talked about politics and the climate like friends, all while they burned a hole in me with their eyes.

Octavian's grandfather and father had chosen not to come to dinner. They had gone out instead. I kept waiting for the Duke to share something of value with my Master, but so far I had not heard anything of any substance.

"Jackson, why don't you go get cleaned up and wait in your bedroom for the Duke?"

"Yes, Master."

"We have some business to discuss while you are preparing."

I nodded that I had heard him as I stood up and pushed my chair back under the table.

"Are you not going to join us?" the Duke asked my Master.

"I will be there in spirit," Octavian said. "I'm afraid that I'm not feeling well enough to . . . show you how to Master that one."

I smiled to myself as I left the dining room and headed down the hallway towards my bedroom. There was no doubt in my mind that Octavian was going to be in the room watching, but the Duke would never know that.

I had showered and was lying naked on the bed when the door finally opened. The Duke strutted inside like a peacock. He closed the door behind him.

"Leave it open," I asked him.

"Why?"

"In case my Master changes his mind."

"Very well." The American opened the door and began undressing. He was still wearing his suit from the summit.

"Have you missed me?" I asked flirtatiously.

"More than you can ever know." He loosened his necktie while staring at me like a hungry lion stared at a gazelle. "Did you miss this?" he asked as he pushed his trousers and boxer briefs to the carpet to reveal his big cock.

"I did, until I met Octavian," I answered honestly.

"He got a cock like this one?" he asked as he pulled his dress shirt over his head.

"Similar."

"Similar smaller?"

"No," I answered flatly.

"That's a shame."

"Not for me."

The Duke walked around to the side of the bed in all of his naked glory. "Let me re-introduce you to the Baron."

"Oh, the Baron and I are old friends," I said as I rolled over onto my back, stretched out and lay with my head over the edge of the mattress in front of him.

He was easily able to slide the Baron into my mouth. Looking down at me, he placed his hand on the side of my face as I deep throated his big cock. "I purposely didn't shower after work, because I know how much you like that."

I made a humming noise to let him know that I appreciated what he was saying. I sucked on his hard column of flesh and savored the salty-sweet taste of his skin. He was already mostly as hard as he was going to get and producing some very thick man-honey.

I sucked the pre-cum from the Duke's fuck stick as he started to move it up and down my throat. I did love a man who knew how to fuck, whether it was a mouth or an ass, either was impressive. And the Duke knew how to fuck.

Using my hands to stroke the monster at the base, I happened to see the cushion on the chair in the corner depress. My new Master was here! I immediately doubled my efforts. I did not want to let Octavian down.

"I see that he has given your mouth a real workout," the Duke said to me as he pumped his hips back and forth. "You could not take all of the Baron's length last year."

I pushed on his crotch and slowly pulled his big dick out of my mouth so that I could talk. I shot a quick glance over towards the empty seat in the room where I knew Octavian was sitting. "My Master has stretched out many of my holes for his pleasure."

"Let's hope that he hasn't ruined your asshole."

"Why don't you try it and see?" I told him as I dipped his wick back into my hungry hole.

"I better, before I bust a nut down your throat."

I hummed in agreement around his hot piece of meat.

The Duke pulled the Baron out of my mouth and gently slapped me across the face with him once in each direction. "Up onto the bed on all fours. I'm going to give you what you want, Jackson."

I scrambled onto the bed onto my hands and knees, grabbing a tube of lube off of the nightstand on my way. The Duke knelt behind me. He spread my legs with his knee and got between them as he lubed his big tool.

He placed one hand on my hip and held the base of his cock with the other one. The Duke guided my ass back while he adjusted his hips to hit his goal.

I opened for him like a flower does for a bee. His hot cock head burrowed its way into my anal ring until I stretched out over his hard bone. It took my breath away for a second, but I was able to recover way faster than when Octavian did the same thing.

The Duke pulled me down and back until he was lying on the bed and I was sitting on his lap. He adjusted his position under me. His long cock prodded my prostate and snuck its way up into my ass until he was completely inside me.

"Fuck! That's what I've been missing." He took a long sniff of me, his nostrils flaring widely.

"Your dick does make me take notice," I admitted, falling into my southern dialect.

"Then you are going to love this . . ."

The Duke began to fuck me by bouncing me up and down on his dick. He kept one hand on my shoulder and the other one on my hip so that he could direct me either to be still while he pounded me from below or to bounce as he kept still.

He was very limber and energetic for such a big man. I was soon sweating profusely as he drilled his cock into me again and again.

"What information did you tell my Master when I left you alone?" I finally asked him. I was milking his cock with my ass muscles and figured that he couldn't stand the pressure much longer.

"I told him a few things, but I'm betting that he already knows them."

He seemed quite smug with himself, even though I couldn't see his face. Either way, it just pissed me off. "Well, that's not fair."

"I got your sweet ass anyway, didn't I?"

"You sure got it now . . ."

"*Fuuuuccccckkkkkk!*" he groaned as he lost his shit.

I settled down onto his legs as he pumped me full of his man-juice. I was breathing hard and still determined to get something out of him before the night was over.

The Duke pulled out of me and rolled over onto his back beside me.

I lay down on my side looking at him. I couldn't help but notice that it appeared that my Master had left his position in the chair. He had probably slipped out of the room when we weren't paying attention. The depression in the seat cushion was no longer there.

"Wow! You never disappoint, do you? Your ass is just as fantastic as I remember."

"I do my best."

"I thought your new Master was even bigger than me?"

"He is."

"Yet your ass is still just as tight as a Servant on the first day of his Service."

"And it still will be later today after you are finished trying to pound me into submission."

"You truly are a miraculous person, Jackson."

"The only miracle is that we both wound up in Zurich at the same time."

"I guess you wouldn't consider becoming my Servant now that you are hooked up with that rich freak, would you?"

"Don't call him that. Octavian is a great man."

"I didn't mean any offense, but you could go out in public with me . . ."

"You would be surprised by what I can do with my big man."

"I would be surprised if he could do this . . ." the Duke informed me as he rolled onto his knees. His cock was red and engorged with blood again.

How have I been so fortunate to attract the attention of these two studs who could reload so quickly?

The Duke stood on the bed and pulled me to my feet. He lifted my six-foot three frame like I weighed nothing as he placed my back against the wall above the headboard.

"Put your legs on my shoulders," he ordered.

I did as I was directed while he pushed his big cock back inside me. The Duke cupped my ass cheeks as his upper body pressed me against the wall. His hips undulated back and forth. The man knew how to fuck and he definitely did it with flair.

"Look at you trying to be all dominant," I said breathily.

"I'm superior to your new Master in almost every way," he bragged. He took another big sniff of me with his larger-than-average nose.

I let out a little chuckle. "I see that you certainly think you are . . ."

He continued to fuck up into me. "I'm smarter, younger, and a better fuck than he is."

"Oh, yeah? What do you know?"

The Duke put his face close to mine and whispered, "I would tell you, but this place is probably bugged."

"No way," I assured him. "Octavian is a freak about his security. He would never let anyone know what goes on in here."

There was a moment of silence between us. I let it fester, because if he became uncomfortable, he might just talk. The Duke finished me off from below and let out his pet phrase again.

We lay on the bed for a while, recovering, before he was ready to go again. He wanted to lie on his back and let me do the work as I rode him. That was fine by me, because I had the control while in that position. I used it to my advantage.

"The secret obviously involves the Chinese."

"Of course."

"They have something that the Americans don't."

He smiled below me.

"Some kind of new tech," I hypothesized.

"A new weapon," he whispered.

I thought about that for a minute while I bounced on his big cock. "Is the Chinese weapon something they would likely use?"

"Yes."

"Would it be helpful to have this technology for our use?"

"By our, do you mean the Americans or the Swiss?"

"I am American and always will be."

"But you are beholden to your Master."

"I am not beholden to him, just subservient to him."

"What if he asks you about the weapon, you will not be able to not tell him. This very room may be bugged." The Duke had already assumed that I was going to keep his secret without even asking me.

"What kind of weapon?" I asked carefully.

He put his finger up to his lips in the sign for *hush.*

"Then I will lean down where you can whisper into my ear." I showed him how this would work as I continued to grind on his long fuck tool.

The Duke considered me for a long moment.

He finally whispered, "An EMP."

"Electro-magnetic pulse? That's not new technology, is it?"

"Look who is well-informed," he said with a bit of awe in his voice. "No, it's not new, but they have found a way to make it smaller and lighter."

I never knew how big it was to begin with, so this news didn't seem so revealing to me.

"They have been able to put it in the nose of a missile or a torpedo. But what is really impressive is that they have one that is hand-held and can be carried into battle."

"How very clever of them."

"They are surprising sometimes."

"And how were you able to learn about this top-secret weapon?"

He pulled his head back from me, smiled, and said, "I have my ways."

This had to be very valuable news to Octavian. I would have to tell him as soon as I was able. Since I got the impression that the Duke was done telling me secrets, I needed to finish with the Duke so that I could speak to Octavian. "Speaking of the missile or torpedo . . ."

"Oh, you want me to get back to pleasuring you?"

"If you don't mind . . ."

The Duke lost his shit again after a few minutes. I was exhausted and wanted nothing more than to talk to Octavian, but I played the game so that he wouldn't suspect what I had planned.

I showed the Duke to his bedroom and introduced him to Joaquim. He seemed delighted to have another marked man's attention, although he would probably wait till the morning to fuck him. I locked the door from the outside, since I didn't want either of them to see Octavian in his invisibility.

I went straight to the shower in my Master's bathroom to scrub the Duke off of me. I was just scrubbing myself clean when I felt Octavian's hands on my ass.

"Are you still mine, little one?"

"Always, Master."

"Do you have anything to tell me, Jackson?"

"You will never believe what I have for you, Master."

"You are my secret weapon, Jackson, so I'm not surprised that you have something for me. I will wait for you in the bed."

"Yes, Master." I started to soap and pull on my dick. I wanted to be able to see Octavian when I told him the news.

CHAPTER TWENTY-FIVE

Excerpt from the journal of Jackson Jurgovan.

June 28, 2019
In the home of Octavian Segunda.
I did not expect to be in Switzerland so long.
I did not expect to find my true Master either.
I did not expect the Duke to find me here in Switzerland.
I had a lot of expectations after my time in The Service, but they were all just blown out of the water. Karma has a way of giving you what you want when you didn't even know that you wanted it.

Octavian let my old friend, the Duke, have me for the night in hopes that he might spill something to me about the summit.

I had forgotten what a great fuck the Duke was, but he still does not do for me what my Master does.

Octavian's plan had worked. I have news for him and can't wait to tell him.

"Master," I said breathlessly when I saw him reclining on his bed. His cock was rock hard, as was mine.

"My Servant."

"I am honored by you, Master."

"It is I who am the honored one, Jackson. You must be tired. Let's go to sleep."

I was surprised. "Yes, Master."

"But, you do have something for me, don't you, Jackson?"

"Of course, Master."

"That's my man!" he said excitedly. "I will be happy to

hear your news over breakfast tomorrow."

I marveled at his patience, but was too tired to do anything but fall right to sleep against his hot body.

I woke to an empty bed, but quickly slid out and got dressed. I was soon in the dining room, joining Octavian and his relatives at breakfast.

"Good morning, Jackson," they said to me as I entered.

"Morning."

Octavian informed me, "The Duke has left for his hotel and the conference has cancelled the morning session."

"Look who has all the news this morning," I quipped as I took a seat at the table.

"Careful," Octavian warned me.

"Sorry, Master." I took a big bite from my piece of toast.

"So, Octavian tells us that you have news, Jackson," his father prompted me.

"I do."

"Did your amazing ass just draw it out of that man, darling?" his grandfather asked shadily.

"I really had to work for it," I said in my defense.

"Nice work if you can get it," Octavian said under his breath. "All right, out with it, Jackson."

I told Octavian and his relatives exactly what the Duke had said last night. I had remembered it word for word, like my new Master had taught me, so I repeated it now.

Octavian was all smiles. "That is excellent intel, my Servant."

"I thought you might like that, Master." I continued to eat.

"I am very proud of you, Jackson."

I blushed under his praise. "Thank you, Master."

"There is one last session of the conference today and then you will be finished with your first mission."

"And we will celebrate, Master?" I watched the big man as

he drank from his coffee cup. My cock was hard as fuck.

"Of course. What would you like to do?"

"I would like to go to Romania for a few days, if we can."

Octavian looked shocked. "Of course we can. Why do you want to?"

"It is the birthplace of my new Master and I want to know everything about him."

Octavian chuckled and said, "It will be interesting for me to see it as a visible person for a change."

I knew what that meant!

Octavian continued, "Father, Grandfather, would you like to accompany us back to the homeland?"

"Not this time, Octavian. We will let you show young Jackson the sites without worrying about us."

I was just finishing my coffee when Octavian looked at me and said, "You will need to be invisible for this afternoon, Jackson, so go get on top of my bed and be prepared to get fucked." His tone practically sizzled with lust.

"I might need to be invisible for a long time, Master."

"You might need to be punished, as well."

"Oh, for God's sake, the two of you just go fuck already," his grandfather said to us.

"Yeah, what he said," I said to Octavian as I stood up and headed out of the dining room.

Three hours later, I was full of my Master's sperm and headed to the conference as an invisible man. I had been careful not to use any toiletry with any scent to it, but I was still worried about the Duke's sense of smell.

My entry into the room was easy enough, so I took up a perch in the alcove and waited. The American diplomats came in about twenty minutes later, including the Duke. They seemed agitated about something, but I did not learn anything that helped me understand their mood.

When the chime sounded, the room cleared out. The Duke was one of the last men to leave and before he did, I saw him turn back towards the empty room and breathe in heavily. His face did not change, but he turned and left without incident.

Taking a huge exhalation, I sat down on the carpet and waited. The Americans returned back to the room about an hour and a half later. I had eaten and used the bathroom while they were gone.

The Duke looked especially agitated, while the other men seemed to be in high spirits. They must have won some key point in the diplomatic talks with the Chinese.

The men started to eat the lunch that had been prepared for them, but I noticed that the Duke was pacing instead of eating. He seemed to constantly be smelling the air in my direction and I contemplated moving, but did not want to give myself away.

The tension in the room seemed to continue to grow until most of the men had finished their lunch and were just sitting around talking. I badly wanted to move to another location, but the Duke would not turn his head away from my position.

"Let me have the room."

It seemed that many of the men had not even heard the Duke. He had still not turned his attention away from my position.

He slammed his hand on the table to get their attention. "Let me have the room!"

The room went silent immediately. The men were still for a few seconds and then started to filter out of the room, talking about the Duke's erratic behavior. The room slowly cleared out. The Duke continued to stare directly at my position.

Once we were alone, I saw the Duke's hand reach for a pitcher of water on the table seconds before I shifted to the side. He quickly grabbed the pitcher, moved to the side of the table, and lunged for me.

I moved away from the splashing water just as it hit the wall behind where I had been standing. The Duke was between me and the door. I would have to go the long way around the conference table and try to sneak out of the door somehow.

The Duke followed after me, staring at my footprints in the thick carpet. Then he stopped in place. He looked up like he could see me. He carefully retraced his steps and stood between me and the door on the other side of the table now.

I slowed down to see what he was going to do as I approached him. I stood still so that he couldn't see my footsteps. Deciding to rush him and get through the door, I took off towards the side of him.

The Duke reached for something on the table, held it in his palm, and raised his hand up to his head. He blew hard on his hand and a black dust cloud appeared right in front of me.

I ran into the cloud and recognized it immediately as pepper. My eyes started to burn and tear up. I sneezed hard as the pepper infiltrated my nostrils, but I kept going. I reached the door and pushed my way through it even as I heard the Duke exclaim his signature yell.

I was free! My Master would not be happy with my inability to stay hidden, but at least the Duke had no proof that I had been there. I quickly made my way out of the building and into the car.

Daniel was surprised to see me so early.

"Will you take me home, please, Daniel?"

The driver handed me a card. *Yes, Jackson.*

Daniel started the car as I texted Octavian. I told him what had happened and that I was coming home to him. I did not get a response.

Once back in Octavian's house, I quietly entered his study.

I wasn't sure whether he was on video with the conference or not, so I didn't say anything.

"We are still on break, my Servant."

"Master, I have failed you," I said to him as I dropped to my knees and bowed my head.

Octavian came over to me and pressed my head against his stomach and held me there. "You have not failed me, Jackson. I have asked a tremendous amount of you and you have delivered."

"Seriously, Master?" I looked up to see his face. He was not mad at me. My cock was not even close to being hard, but that was not going to last for very long.

"It took me a lifetime of practice to be invisible, Jackson, and you have done it in weeks. I could never be disappointed with you."

"Master is too kind." My cock started to harden as I breathed in his smell.

"He will be here shortly, Jackson."

"The Duke?" I asked in surprise. I thought I was free of him.

"Yes. He will press his advantage, I am afraid."

"What does he want?"

"We shall see. Go shower and get cleaned up so that he can see you when he arrives."

"Yes, Master." I hesitated before leaving. I wanted to apologize again, but was unsure what to say.

"*Now*, Jackson," Octavian said firmly.

"Master, I—"

"You will do as I command, Servant, or you will pay the price," he said resolutely.

I will gladly pay the price . . .

CHAPTER TWENTY-SIX

Excerpt from the journal of Jackson Jurgovan.

June 29, 2019
In the home of Octavian Segunda.
I messed up
Somehow the Duke was able to smell me at the conference and made every effort to prove that I was there. He tried to throw water on me and then forced me into a cloud of black pepper.
I just barely escaped.
I thought Octavian would have been furious with me, but he was not. He has been very sweet about it.
We are preparing for a visit from the Duke. Octavian says that he will press his advantage.
I'm not sure what was about to happen and that was frightening.
I was cleaning myself up so that I could be visible when he arrives.
On a brighter note, I have asked Octavian to take me on a trip to Romania for a few days and he has agreed. I am looking forward to seeing his home country and being away with him.

A couple of hours later, I was clean and visible again when Konju came into Octavian's study. He bowed deeply.

"Master, the Duke is here and would like to see you."

"Give me a minute, Konju, and then show him to the study," Octavian said while beginning to don his bandages and gloves.

"Yes, Master." Konju headed for the door.

I jumped up and helped Octavian get completely covered. It would not do well for one of the bandages to reveal an empty hole where skin and bone should have been.

"What will happen, Master?"

"We are about to see, Jackson. Sit down. You are making me nervous."

"Yes, Master." I took a seat on one of the couches facing the door.

A soft knock on the door preceded Konju appearing with the Duke in tow. "The Duke, Master."

"And to what do we owe the pleasure of this visit?" Octavian quickly asked as he stood up behind his desk.

I chose not to stand.

The Duke's eyes blazed at me as he crossed the room. He shook Octavian's hand before taking the seat in the chair in front of my Master's desk.

"I know your secret, Segunda."

"And what secret would that be?"

I was amazed at how much calm Octavian's voice carried.

"I know you have been spying on us at the conference," the Duke blurted out.

Octavian chuckled and asked, "And how would I do that?"

"You sent Jackson in to listen on our conversations."

"Oh, you saw Jackson there?"

"Yes—no—well, I'm not sure how you are doing it, but I am positive that Jackson was in that room today."

"You have proof of that?" I challenged him.

He snapped his head in my direction. "I saw you," he said in a growl. He turned back to my Master and said, "I don't know whether you are using some type of new cloaking tech or what, but he was there."

"And what would you like from me?"

The Duke showed his teeth as he smiled broadly. "I'm sure that the international community would find this information very interesting. Heck, I think your competitors here in Zurich would find your tactics to be criminal, at the very least."

"And yet, you have no proof," Octavian replied with his hands out to his sides.

"I don't think I need it. The Chinese would probably be very interested in your cloaking technology, even if I have no proof of it. You would suddenly become very interesting to them."

I could see his point. "Fuck you!" I said with venom.

"No, fuck you, Jackson, and that is exactly what I am going to do."

"Make your point," Octavian commanded.

The Duke leaned back in his chair and steepled his fingers in front of him. "You give me Jackson as my Servant and I will not tell the Chinese or the Americans."

My heart sank. I felt like I had failed Octavian miserably. I stood, walked to the front of Master's desk, leaned my ass against the heavy wood and faced the Duke.

"My answer is no. Jackson?" Octavian's tone gave nothing away.

"Fuck, no," I spit out. "Can't you see that no one wants you here, Duke? I would rather never get fucked again than have to be your Servant."

The Duke sprang with surprising quickness. He grabbed me around the throat, spittle foaming in the corners of his mouth. "You will fucking do whatever I tell you to do."

I tried to talk but couldn't. I put my hands on his hand, trying to pry it off of my neck.

He lifted me off of the desk and into the air.

I struggled against his grip. Out of the corner of my eye, I could see Octavian stand up and start to remove his clothes and bandages.

"This is not going to go well for you," he growled at the Duke.

I felt the duke's grip relax as he watched Octavian go invisible. Taking advantage of my opening, I spun, pulled his arm around his back and shoved him into the bookcase. The Duke's head broke the blue octopi's tank and when he stumbled back, Sabi was sucked onto his face. Water rushed into the room with the sound of breaking glass.

"Nicely done, Jackson . . . and Sabi."

"Master, this is all my fault—"

"Silence. I won't hear any more of that. Help me get Sabi off of him, before he hurts my pet."

I looked down at the Duke, who was clawing at the octopus on his face.

Octavian put his knee on the Duke's chest and we pulled Sabi from his face. The blue and gold octopus quickly wrapped his tentacles around my hands and arms. It was a weird feeling having the suckers stuck to my skin.

"Put him in with the black octopus over there," Octavian told me as he nodded in the direction of one of the other tanks.

I followed his directions as I listened to him threaten our guest. Sabi was attached to me and didn't seem to want to go in the tank with the other octopus. It took me quite a while to get him detached from my arms.

"I could have you thrown off a mountain and no one would find you for years."

"What are you?" the Duke asked with a small amount of terror in his voice.

"Your worst nightmare. You will obviously keep quiet about everything that you have seen here or think you know, or Jackson and I will be visiting you in the middle of the night to silence you. You will never see us coming and you will never be safe, even in broad daylight, surrounded by an army of security. We will slip right past them."

"You are invisible, too, Jackson?" he asked me, his voice quivering.

"You will die before you even know we are in the same room with you, Duke," I answered him firmly.

"Your business will turn to shit, your relationships will fall apart, your life will be shit," Octavian threatened.

"I will—will not say anything."

"You better pray you don't. Now, get out of my house. I never want to see you or hear your name again."

My cock was hard, so I could watch Octavian remove his knee from the middle of the Duke's chest. He grabbed him by the shoulders, jerked him onto his feet and threw him towards the door of the study. Of course, the Duke couldn't see him, so he seemed quite stunned by this invisible force that was manhandling him.

"I will leave, don't worry."

"We will be watching."

The Duke finally pried his eyes off of where Octavian had been to look at me. He opened his mouth to say something.

"Get the fuck out," I said firmly. "You are not wanted here."

I'm not sure how Konju and Master's security guards knew that there was a problem, but they soon appeared at the door. Since Octavian was invisible, I realized that I had to assume control.

"Please have the Duke escorted from the property, Konju. He is never welcome here again."

"Yes, Master Jackson."

The Duke hesitated to move, but then received an invisible push from behind. I could see that Octavian was menacing him, but neither he nor the security guards coming at him could. Both big men grabbed the Duke by the upper arms and carried him from the room.

"I will be back to clean up this mess, Master," Konju told Octavian, although he couldn't see him at all.

"I think we just did," I said to the room.

"I'm sure of it," Octavian added.

CHAPTER TWENTY-SEVEN

Excerpt from the journal of Jackson Jurgovan.

June 30, 2019
In the home of Octavian Segunda.
Today was very exciting.
The Duke tried to blackmail Octavian. He would tell the authorities our secret if Octavian didn't give him me as a Servant.
Luckily for me, Octavian was having none of it.
It got physical, and even Octavian's pet, Sabi, got in on the act. I was thrilled beyond belief that Octavian would have fought for me and risked everything to keep me. I am beyond his.
The Duke left in a huff, but I'm pretty sure he got the point. If he ever opened his mouth, we would be there to shut it for him. I have no doubt that he would not have been believed, even if he had told someone. He will always be looking over his shoulder for us.
I vowed not to ever let this situation happen again. It was because of my carelessness that the Duke figured out Octavian's secret, even though he thought it was some kind of high-tech cloaking device that made him invisible. I never want that to happen again.
Octavian seemed proud of me after we retired for the night. He fucked me hard twice before I feel asleep against his chest. My ass was burning from his giant tool, but I was completely satisfied to belong to him that I barely noticed.
Master had promised to take me to Romania for a visit to his homeland and he told me that we were leaving tomorrow. I loved that Octavian was so attentive to me and would just drop everything to take me away for the week. He was the most amazing man that I have ever met.

I had something special planned for the trip, but I didn't want to jinx it yet by writing about it. More to come . . .

By the time Octavian and I arrived at the airport in Zurich, he had just fucked me hard. I was completely naked and Octavian was dressed to the nines in a black suit with a red shirt open at the neck.

I headed right for the stairs of the sleek private plane, still not comfortable being naked in a room full of NOMARs, even though I was invisible. From the top step, I turned and saw Octavian shaking hands with the flight crew. It was the first time that they had ever seen him and he seemed to be soaking up their attention.

I was happy to give that to him. If nothing more transpired between us except for him fucking me and becoming visible, then I would be very happy. I was still smiling to myself as I entered the plane and found a seat.

"What is so funny, Servant?" Octavian's voice was absolutely smoldering. He had come onto the plane as silently as a cat.

"I am happy for you, Master."

"And I am happy with you, Jackson."

"I have screwed up so many things for you . . ."

"Not at all. You have done exactly what I asked of you and so much more." He took a seat beside me.

"Thank you for this trip, Master." I heard the doors close ahead of us.

"You are welcome. I am excited to show you my homeland."

We were soon in the air and it was not much longer before I was on my knees in front of my Master.

"You do that well, Servant."

My mouth was full of Octavian's giant cock, so there was no way to respond except to hum around his hummer. I was so proud of myself for being able to swallow almost two-thirds of him, but I had to completely concentrate to keep from gagging.

Master leaned back on the head rest and said, "Yes, I know. I inspire you."

I laughed to myself as I suctioned my mouth up his long thick cock and sucked the spit off of the end of his beautiful cock head.

"I like you inspired, my Servant."

I ran my wide tongue from his balls up to that beautiful cock head.

He cleared his throat and in his best American accent, he said, "Master, I will continue to service you as long as you will have me."

Pulling his ball sack out of the opening in the front of his suit pants, I immediately sucked one of his fat balls into my mouth.

"I've never met a man who fills me up like you do." He started to chuckle and fell out of his American accent.

I sucked the other ball into my mouth.

"I can't get enough of your big tool inside me." Now, he disassembled into full-fledged laughter.

I spit out his balls and looked up into his face with humor on my lips. "Master thinks he is funny."

"Master knows that he is funny and speaking of not being able to get enough of this big tool inside you . . ." He reached down and pulled me to my feet in one swift movement.

We were alone in the cabin of his private plane, but I'm not sure Octavian would have cared even if we weren't. He pulled his legs together and guided me onto his lap. I stood above him, reached around behind me, and guided his massive meat-missile to my backdoor.

"You are lucky that I love this cock of yours so much, Master."

"I am the lucky one."

"You'll be lucky not to ruin that beautiful suit of yours."

I pushed my hips down and impaled myself on his cock. My eyes closed and I held my breath as the pain threatened to overwhelm me. Talking internally to myself, I recited that the pleasure was going to be worth the pain over and over.

Octavian's dick was so large, both in length and girth, that I never thought it would fit inside me, yet it found a way every time. His giant cockhead relentlessly rammed into places never visited by men before. The wide girth of his steel-hard shaft kept my anal ring spread wide open as it slowly slid inside me. When I finally reached his short hairs and knew that he was completely inside of me, I opened my eyes and exhaled.

"I am the lucky one," I whispered.

"I am the lucky one," my Master repeated. "There is nothing like your ass, Jackson."

"It is yours, Master."

"And I can do anything I want to it, Servant?"

"Yes, Master. Anything."

"I want to fuck it so hard," he told me as he pushed my hips up and quickly pulled them back down again.

His fucking left me speechless, which was probably for the best, because we were right in the middle of it when one of the flight crew walked in from the cabin.

Octavian's employee blushed immediately, looked down, and stammered, "I'm sorry, Mr. Segunda. I-I-"

My Master continued to fuck me hard without even breaking rhythm. "It's okay, Francis. What do you need?"

"We are preparing to descend, sir."

I'm sure that this looked very strange to Francis. I could picture in my mind what the scene entailed. All he could see was Octavian sitting in a chair with his cock hard as a beam and pointed straight to heaven. Octavian's big hands were in the air in front of him and he was moving them up and down.

"Very good. I will strap into my seat in a minute."

"Yes, sir." Francis left without even a look back over his shoulder.

"Yes, sir," I repeated breathily as I rode Octavian's merry-go-round pole over and over. I could feel the large veins on the outside of Master's shaft as I slid up and down over them. The sensations they were giving to me were unbelievable.

"You are mine, aren't you, Jackson?" he asked in his husky voice that went right to my balls.

"I am yours, Master."

"You won't leave me, will you?"

"I will only go once you are done with me, Master. I have no will but to pleasure you."

"Now, that makes me a lucky man." He increased the speed and power that he was fucking me with, causing both of us to come within the minute. I was so lost in the moment that I had no idea where my cum splashed or how much even poured from my cock. I was in total ecstasy.

I was absolutely spent as Octavian poured me into the seat beside him and strapped me into it. In my head, I could picture what the flight crew might see if they were watching—Octavian's big dick exploding into thin air and then the hot cum just disappearing from view.

"You are about to land in Romania, Jackson."

"Your homeland, Master."

"Yes."

"And maybe mine. I'll probably never know."

"We shall see," he answered mysteriously.

"How, Master?"

"They say that you can feel it in your bones and in your blood. Your homeland does something to you. It makes your body sing."

"The fucking should be amazing then, if both of our bodies are singing, Master."

"Exactly what I was thinking, Jackson. Same page, as usual."

CHAPTER TWENTY-EIGHT

Excerpt from the journal of Jackson Jurgovan.

July 1, 2019
At the airport in Bucharest, Romania
Today has been amazing. Octavian and I arrived in Romania on his private plane, which allowed us time to fuck all the way.

I left the plane, invisible, while my Master was large and in charge — moving us and our luggage to a nearby limousine.

I was in the back of the limousine looking out the window at Bucharest when I felt it for the first time. There was a tingling on the right side of my face. I reached up and rubbed it, but it did not stop. I turned my head to face the front seat and the tingling moved to the front of my face — my nose and upper lip tingling like crazy.

I looked at the back of the driver's head and the tingling stopped. Instead a picture appeared in my brain. It was a doctor's office. The doctor was handing over some bad news. I felt his pain. I felt his fear. I felt his worry.

Something told me that his name was Daneill. Why would that thought pop into my head?

The picture in my brain changed to one of a kitchen table. There was a woman and three kids. I knew immediately that this was Daneill's wife and kids. Something told me that this scene had not played out yet, but would in the very near future. He was telling his family the news. It was not going to go well.

I could feel the devastation that Daneill would feel.

"Daneill, I am sorry for your condition," I said from the back seat.

Octavian's head whipped in my direction. I'm not sure if he was more stunned by the fact that I was talking while invisible, that I knew our driver's name without asking, or that I was speaking Romanian.

"How — how?" the driver stumbled.

"In my position, I have access to a tremendous amount of information."

"Thank you, Mr. Segunda."

Daneill obviously thought that Octavian was speaking to him, because as far as he knew, he only had one passenger. Smartly, Octavian had covered his mouth with his hand.

"How long have you worked for me, Daneill?" I asked him. I wasn't sure he was an employee, but I thought I knew Octavian well enough that he would not trust just anyone to drive him.

"Ten years, sir. But this is the first time I have actually driven you anywhere."

He probably had driven Octavian many times, but did not even realize it. The car pulled into a palatial estate surrounded by a very high metal fence. Daneill stopped at the guard house.

"You have Mr. Segunda?" the guard asked.

"Yes," he answered as he flipped on the overhead light in the back of the limousine.

The security guard looked shocked when he saw Octavian for the very first time. "Mr. Segunda?"

"Yes," Octavian answered.

The guard looked confused by what to do or say next.

"Aren't you going to scan my prints, Elo?"

I was impressed that Octavian knew his name.

"Oh, right. Yes, sir," the guard said as he ducked into the security hut to retrieve the fingerprint scanner. He returned to the back window where Octavian had stuck his hand out of the window.

Since no one had ever seen Octavian's face before, he had come to rely on his employees to recognize his signet ring, which he wore at all times when he was bandaged. It was a beautiful silver ring with a black lacquered top. Easily identifiable on the top, was Octavian's mark—an elegant octopus shaped like the letter O and his eight arms each forming the letter S.

"It is you," Elo said in awe as the scanner confirmed Octavian's identity.

"Yes, it's me. You can see the signet ring, can't you? Now, open the gate."

"Yes, sir." Elo hurried inside to press the button, activating the mechanism that allowed the heavy iron gate to open.

Daneill drove forward down the circled drive, stopping in front of the entrance to the mansion.

I said, "Do not worry about your family, Daneill. I will make sure that they are comfortable financially for the rest of their lives."

Octavian smiled while he looked at me intently.

"Mr. Segunda, I don't know what to say."

"I thank you for your years of service, Daneill."

The driver left the car and opened the back door for us. "I am speechless, Mr. Segunda."

I snuck out of the car before Octavian, who shook the driver's hand and told him he was welcome.

"How did you know?" Octavian asked me as we walked towards the front door. Daneill was too busy with the bags to pay attention to us.

"Something has happened, Master," I said simply.

A butler opened the door for us before we arrived to it. He greeted Octavian and left the door open for Daneill.

The house was absolutely beautiful—fully furnished with no expense being spared. It was very different from Octavian's Swiss house. This was a traditional house with lots of exposed wood and stone.

Octavian and I retired to the master bedroom as soon as he had taken care of issuing orders to the household staff.

He shut the door before asking me, "How did you do that?"

"I think something has happened to me, Master."

"Wait, I want you mounted on my cock before you answer." Octavian started stripping off his clothing.

I started to search for lube. I wasn't going to miss a chance to be fucked by my dream man, even though he had just pulled out of me a little more than an hour ago.

Octavian lay down in the middle of the bed and started to stroke his massive member while he watched me grab lube from the night stand drawer.

"I am not the first Servant that Master has had in this bedroom," I said as I shook the tube of lube at him before throwing it on the bed. I stepped onto the bed and carefully walked to the middle where I straddled my Master. "This house is beautiful, by the way. Is it your family home?"

"No. I built this house a few years ago to stay in when I come home," he told me as he guided me down to my knees. He held out two thick fingers together and I poured lube on them.

Master quickly inserted those thick digits into my ass as he expertly finger-blasted me. I poured more lube into my palm, reached behind me, and started to slick up his meat rocket.

I couldn't wait to have him inside me again. Octavian finished fingering my ass and wiped his hand on the sheets. My ass felt like something was missing when he wasn't planted to the hilt inside me. Rising up slightly, I placed his soft cock head against my rosebud.

I was expecting to be in control, but my Master put me in my place. He pushed his pelvis up at the same time that he pushed my hips down, causing his gigantic cock to push inside me with force.

I closed my eyes and threw back my head as the wonderful sensation of my anal ring being widened to its limit combined with the searing pain of his penetration.

"So good, Jackson," Octavian said as he slid the last few inches inside me.

I was unable to speak, so I just moaned my appreciation to him. I could have sworn that every time Octavian fucked me, that his cock found places inside me where he had never gone before.

He stroked my chest as I got used to his sheer size and girth. When I finally opened my eyes and looked down at him, he was smiling at me.

"Now, what do you mean that something has happened to you?"

I went to open my mouth to answer him, but he decided to start pumping his cock up and down into my ass. I had to take a moment and swallow before answering.

"When we landed and got in the car, I felt a strange tingling sensation on my cheek."

"Like a feather touching you?" He slammed his cock to the short hairs in me particularly hard.

"That is no feather, Master, but yes."

He long-dicked me again, chuckling at my joke.

"I turned forward and the tingling moved to the front of my face. I was looking directly at the back of Daneill's head."

"Ok." He pounded me from below several more times.

"And then, I don't know. This picture just popped into my head."

He fucked me fast and furious before slowing again to ask, "And what? You just knew things about him?"

"Yeah. I knew he was sick and that it was terminal. I knew his name and that he was planning on telling his family to-night. I could feel his emotions."

Octavian now rhythmically stroked my ass with his big cock. He looked like he was deep in thought. "Strange," he finally said.

"It was. And I could even see how the future was going to go when he told his family. Now I'm wondering why I couldn't read the security guard or the butler."

"We will have to see if this is a one-time thing or if it happens again."

"Yes, Master."

"I'm glad you have remembered that I am your Master and that you are here to serve me, Jackson." He quickly moved his hips up and down, making my asshole fly up and down his hard shaft. He was super-heating my skin while he had me stretched to my limits.

"It is never far from my mind, Master," I moaned as he sent me into another strata of pleasure.

"On all fours, Servant. I want to finish you from behind."

"Yes, Master." I quickly scrambled to obey him.

I had my head buried in the pillow as Octavian drove his cock home and busted his nut deep inside me.

I release you from the curse . . .

The thought just popped into my head while Octavian was continuing to slowly fuck me from behind, despite having already ejaculated inside me.

But, is that what I really want?

Octavian slowed his progress further and pressed himself to my back. I loved the feeling of his weight being on me.

Would Octavian even still want me if he could be visible all the time? Would he even need me?

I listened to his breathing as it returned to normal and he touched me lightly with just his fingertips, absentmindedly stroking my side.

Why would I have the power to change a centuries-old curse?

"That was exceptional, Master."

"You are exceptional, Jackson."

"My bladder is not, however. I have to pee badly."

Octavian shifted his weight to the side of me and I slipped out of the bed and into the bathroom. It was a strange sensation to have his big dick not in my ass. I looked in the mirror on my way by and saw that I was very much invisible.

"Your house is exceptional, though," I said loudly enough for him to hear me from the bathroom.

"It is yours now also," he said.

I started to piss. "Does your family home still stand?"

Octavian walked into the bathroom. "Sort of. It is in shambles. Would you like to see it?"

"Very much."

"I will arrange it."

"Master is most kind to me," I said as we switched places.

"Master is not finished with you yet." His voice was still husky with lust and I salivated at his words.

CHAPTER TWENTY-NINE

E xcerpt from the journal of Jackson Jurgovan.

July 2, 2019

At the home of Octavian Segunda in Bucharest, Romania

Today, I tried to break the curse that haunts Octavian and his family. From what I knew of the curse, it happened when Octavian's forefather was fucking a marked Gypsy.

So, I thought that if he was fucking me in Romania, that it might break the curse. I was hopeful until I saw the butler coming down the hall and he obviously could not see me standing there completely nude.

I have some more thoughts on breaking the curse and will follow up on them today, if possible. I mean, if it means that Octavian will just have to continue to fucking pound me every day and night, then why not continue to try? I will never give up!

Octavian has promised to show me his family's ancestral home today, so I'm looking forward to that. I want to know everything about Octavian Segunda and deepen our bond, although it is already deeper and more meaningful than any I have ever had with a NOMAR.

I woke up early and proceeded to suck on Master's big fuck-stick until he was blowing a hot load of spunk down my throat. He gave me a quick hard fuck from behind as we lay on our sides, before telling me to shower and report to the dining room for breakfast.

I took my time getting ready. Octavian kept my ass full of his cum almost at all times, so keeping clean was going to be a real challenge for me. I decided to wrap myself in bandages so that I could interact with people this morning.

"Ah, there he is," Octavian said when he saw me walk into the dining room. I was covered from head to foot in cloth of some sort so that I could be seen.

There was only the butler in the room. He quickly made me a plate of food and served it to me when he saw me enter.

"Marto, this is my business partner, Jackson," Octavian said to the butler.

"Jackson, Marto has been with me for over twelve years."

"It is nice to meet you, Master Jackson," Marto said with a half bow. "It is wonderful that you convinced Master Segunda to come visit us. It has been way too long."

"Nice to meet you, Marto." I tucked into the plate of eggs, toast, and fried potatoes in front of me.

"Your Romanian is excellent, Master Jackson. You are American, are you not?"

"I am, but I have been taking very intensive lessons from Octavian for several weeks now, so I'm almost an expert."

Octavian shot me a look that told me to be quiet.

"Marto takes care of my house and cars while I am not here." Octavian had obviously finished his breakfast and was in a talkative mood.

My ass was still burning from this morning's hard fuck to be in such a good mood.

Marto said, "And if it is not too impertinent of me to say, Master Segunda. Your skin looks amazing. Almost flawless."

"Thank you, Marto. Jackson has been instrumental in my treatments, and if not for him, I'm afraid I would still be bandaged at this very moment."

"And you suffer from the same affliction as Master does, Master Jackson?"

"I do."

"Perhaps you can work your miracle on yourself then."

"Perhaps. I will make sure that Octavian continues to

improve before I think of myself, of course."

"Of course."

A second man entered the room, carrying a cloche of food on a tray. He was dressed exactly like Marto, so I assumed he was also a butler.

"Sir, if I could introduce Peti to you," Marto said to Octavian.

My face began to tingle. This time, I knew what to do. Swiveling my head, until the tingle centered on the middle of my face, I saw that I was looking straight at Peti as he bowed to my Master.

"I hired him immediately when you informed me that you were coming for a visit," Marto continued.

A picture appeared in my head.

"Nice to meet you, Peti. Where is your family from?"

"I'm from Isai, sir. Nice to meet you, as well," he answered politely.

"Peti, this is my business associate, Jackson. He has a skin condition, so privacy is very important to us."

"I have signed the confidentiality waivers that Marto gave me when I was hired, sir."

"Too bad there were no waivers about stealing," I said.

"Excuse me?" Octavian asked. Both of the butlers' heads snapped in my direction.

I put my fork down on my plate and said, "Peti is stealing from you, Master."

"I am not!" Peti erupted.

"Do you have proof, Jackson, or is this a feeling?"

"He has four pieces of your silver service in his coat pocket right now," I said, crossing my arms and leaning back into the chair away from the table.

Marto immediately jumped at the new butler and opened his jacket to reveal the four items hidden there. "I am so sorry, Master Segunda. This is my fault for hiring him."

"He has helped himself to the money in your petty cash envelope from your desk also, Marto," I added.

"How do you know?" Peti asked loudly to me. "There are no cameras inside here. I checked."

"I just know when someone has done something bad."

"Get him out of here, Marto. And make sure you get the house money back from him."

"Yes, sir." Marto was bigger than Peti, so he had no problem hauling him out of the dining room by the scruff of his jacket.

"Did you get that tingling thing again?" Octavian asked me as soon as the door was closed.

"Yes, Master."

"Huh. Handy."

"Yes, very."

"I wonder why this is happening only here in Romania."

"Me too." I had a suspicion that I might have been Romanian myself, and that would have explained some of my connection to the country and whatever was happening with me.

"Shall we go for a ride to the countryside today, or is there anything here in the city that you want to do?"

"I am only here to serve you, Master. I will do whatever brings you the most pleasure."

"Well, fucking you will bring me the most pleasure, but I suppose we can get both done at the same time, right?"

"Absolutely, Master."

Marto re-entered the dining room and immediately started to apologize to Octavian, who cut him off.

"It is not your fault, Marto. I was even starting to like the guy."

"But Master Jackson was so right about him." Marto had a new look of respect in his eyes when he looked at me. "I found over half of my petty cash in his pants pocket."

"He has a special gift for that sort of thing, don't you,

Jackson?"

"I certainly seem to."

"Marto, we are going to spend the day out. We will return for dinner. I think you should have our traditional pastrami dinner for Jackson tonight. Ask Bardon if he minds cooking it for me."

"He is your chef, sir. He will do as he is commanded."

"At least there is someone who does," I said under my breath, only loud enough for Octavian to hear.

"You will be punished for that," he said firmly while pointing his finger at me. "We will be honored to eat Bardon's feast tonight."

"Yes, sir. I will inform him and it will be done."

"Excellent! Jackson, if you are finished, we can get going."

"I am at your mercy, Master."

"As you always are. Now, get ready to go."

"Shall I go in bandages or invisible, Master?"

"Even though it is July, I think it will be too cold for you to go naked, Jackson. I would think you would want to dress in layers and use bandages for your face. It will get warmer in the afternoon."

"I'll be ready in a little bit, Master."

A half hour later, I was standing in Octavian's garage, marveling at the selection of cars that he kept in Romania for his visits.

"Which one do you like, my Servant?"

"I like them all, Master. Especially if they smell like you."

He winked at me and said, "I think we will take the Audi." He walked towards a car that looked very futuristic. "They only made a couple of these cars."

I saw the name *Audi Lemans Concept* on the back of the car, but I did not know cars well enough to know what that meant. I didn't find out until later that Octavian had paid five million dollars for it.

"Looks fast, Master."

"It is," he said, with a twinkle in his eye. "Just wait."

I slid into the leather passenger's seat and marveled at the futuristic dashboard in front of me. The car did not smell like my Master yet, but I was sure that it would by the end of our trip.

Octavian started the engine and opened the garage doors in one swift movement. He pulled out of the garage and onto the driveway with such precision and power that it took my breath away.

I looked over at him and smiled beneath my bandages.

"This car makes me horny, Servant."

"You are always horny, Master. This car might make you even more horny."

"That's right. I owe you a punishment today, don't I?"

"Yes, Master." I was kinda hoping that he had forgotten, but at the same time, the very thought of being punished by him made me hard as a rock.

"It is a short drive to my family's homestead, Jackson, but long enough for you to give me one of your superior blow jobs on the way."

"Yes, Master!" I'm not sure whether this was a punishment or a reward, but I was quite excited about it. I unbuckled my seat belt and twisted my body around towards him.

We stopped at a red light and Octavian pulled his big joint out of the fly of his jeans like he was well-practiced at it.

I was on him in seconds.

"Wow. Someone is an eager beaver this morning."

"I aim to please, Master," I told him as I settled my head into the small space between the steering wheel and his big body.

Octavian's cock was generating a lot of heat. His skin tasted and smelled like apple-flavored soap. I practiced trying to swallow as much of him as I could, but his constant turning and shifting of the car made it difficult.

I soon had developed a good pace of bobbing up and down on his fuck stick, when Octavian pulled the car onto a dirt and gravel parking lot beside the road surrounded by trees. He came at almost the exact moment that he brought the car to a skidding sliding stop.

Swallowing like I needed his sweet cream to breathe, I sucked him dry before looking up. I looked out the front window to see several food trucks and what looked like a log cabin.

"This is your family home, Master?" I asked in surprise.

"No. This is the place where we get the sacred water from." He looked down at me with an expression that conveyed that I should have already known this. "Are you finished down there?"

"Yes, Master," I answered before chasing the last pearl of his man-juice down his big rod.

"Zip me up. We need to collect some of the water."

I followed his command and then slid out of the car behind him.

Octavian walked with purpose over to the log cabin and came out with two large glass water containers. "The stream is over here," he told me as he set off across the street.

I looked in wonder at what I had thought had been one of those Catholic niches where a saint usually stood. Instead of a saint in this one, there was a pipe that fresh mountain water poured from.

"It is said that if you sprinkle this over your home and possessions that they will always be yours," he told me as he moved his oversized hand under the water and completely diverted the stream right at me.

I squawked with surprise before saying, "I will always be yours, Master."

"Now, you squirt me," he commanded.

"Not the type of squirt I would have chosen," I said lightly as I sprayed him with the water.

"You are bad, Jackson."

"You are mine now, Master."

"I was before," he told me before starting to fill the two glass containers with water.

"If you are hungry, we can eat here," he said later at the car. "This stand is famous for their sausage rolled in pastry. It's Hungarian."

"I do like sausage, Master."

"Yes, you do. Let's get some."

My stomach was full and I was extremely happy with my Master as we got back on the road. Neither of us had much to say as the sports car climbed into the mountains.

The sun was starting to dip down behind the mountains when Octavian pulled the car onto a gravel path lined with ancient trees. The driveway, if it could have been called that, led into the dark forest.

"This is it," he said firmly.

"Hidden from view."

"That was always a plus for my family."

"Yes," I agreed, chuckling.

"Until you came along, Jackson."

"I have brought you into the light, Master?"

"In more ways than you will ever know."

CHAPTER THIRTY

Excerpt from the journal of Jackson Jurgovan.

July 3, 2019
The contents of Octavian Segunda's garage in Bucharest, Romania.
Ducati 1260S motorcycle
Triumph Bonneville Speedmaster motorcycle
Wazuma V8 Quad
Range Rover Phantom
Jaguar F-Type R
Rolls Royce SUV Phev
Bentley Bentayga V8
Dasha Duster
Audi Lemans Concept
Ferreri 812 GTS
Lamborghini Huracan EVO Spyder
Maserati Quattroporte
Honda Ridgeline
Caged Trailor

"We are almost there, Master?" I asked as the sportscar we were riding in plunged down the darkened path in the woods.

"We're here," he said dramatically as the car came to a skidding halt in front of a pile of stones.

The forest was cleared around the house, so I could easily see it, although the dust from the road needed a few seconds to clear before I could see the details.

The house had once been fairly large, but now all that was left of it were stones. The woodwork and iron used in the construction were completely gone as well as the roof and any supporting beams.

I got out of the car, looking at the ruins with disappointment.

"The Segunda family home," Octavian said with a lilt in his voice.

"It looks like it was really grand in its time."

"I believe it was. Do you want to go inside?"

"I do, Master."

We stepped through the arched doorway and into a reception room, where there was once a flight of stairs leading up to the second floor. I only knew that because I saw the holes in the wall going up in a methodical diagonal pattern. I got a strange tingling sensation in my chest as soon as I was inside. I let out a deep breath, but still felt strange.

Octavian had brought one of the bottles of sacred water and was now, sprinkling it in the ruins of his ancestral home.

Each room had thick grass underfoot which was beautifully trimmed short. "Does someone mow this, Master?"

"I believe that one of the local farmers lets his goats and sheep take care of it, Jackson."

"Oh," I said, feeling foolish.

We moved into a larger room to the right. It had what was left of a fireplace and even some scraps of stained glass that had once made up the windows. The tingling in my chest became even more pronounced.

"I've never met someone who wanted to so completely know me," Octavian said as he stared at me.

"You are my everything now, Master. I have to know."

"You amaze me, Jackson." His voice had dropped several octaves.

"Do you think this was a bedroom, Master?" I purposely raised one of my eyebrows at him.

"I believe it was the parlor, Servant, but I like what you are getting at."

We moved into the next room, which was dominated by what was once a gigantic fireplace. He sprinkled the water along the way. I noticed that my body became even more responsive to the house.

"Family room, Master?"

"I would think so, Servant. The bedrooms were probably upstairs at one point, but this room might also have been one," he told me as he led me to a smaller room in the back. He wet down the rocks and grass ahead of him.

"I would like you to fuck me in this room, Master." I dropped to my knees in front of him.

"I am at your service, Jackson." He unzipped his jeans and pulled out my favorite body part.

I quickly grabbed his joint by the root and held it out so that I could try to completely swallow it. He tasted and smelled good, even though I had already blown him in the car. The Octavian smell wafted into my nasal passages as my saliva glands worked overtime to slicken the beast inside my mouth.

As usual, Octavian was almost always ready to go. It did not take too much blowing on his Roman candle, for him to ignite.

"I'm ready to fuck my new Servant in the ruins of my family's ancestral home."

"I am honored to be the recipient of your long . . . history. Pour the centuries of Segunda's into me, Master." I took a final lick of his hot cock and stood up to strip. I was soon on all fours on the thick grass.

Octavian placed the point of his cock on my rosebud. Just using the spit I had left on his dick, he pushed his hips forward and slid his fat joint inside me.

It felt like I was being cleaved in half. The pain was so sharp and biting that I felt light-headed instantly. I made small promises to myself that helped me deal with the pain.

Just wait . . .

The pleasure will be immense . . .

The pain will go completely away . . .

It is worth it . . .

As the pain started to recede, I felt something inside of me shift. The thrumming in my chest moved lower to my crotch and started to intensify. Something was happening.

Master had sunk to his nuts inside of me and decided to light a cigar in celebration. I waited, trying to get used to the large chunk of man-meat that was currently occupying a significant amount of real estate inside my ass. Between the thrumming in my crotch and the blood pulsing in Octavian's cock, it felt like I had a couple of time bombs ticking away inside me.

Octavian clenched his cigar between his teeth, grabbed my hips with both hands and started his fuck-stroke. He was so forceful that it threatened to knock me off of my position on the ground. I felt my cock and balls start to come to life. I would be hard in a minute.

"Master," I moaned to him.

"Tearing you up now, my Servant," he growled back to me.

The tingling sensation in my crotch spread to my ass, warming my skin even as Octavian slammed into my buttocks every few seconds. Suddenly, a thought jumped into my head.

As softly as I could, I said, "As a marked man of Romanian heritage, I countermand the curse put upon the Segunda family."

The tingling sensation started on the top of my head and quickly crashed like a wave as it ran all the way down my body and out of the soles of my feet.

"Whoa. Did you feel that?" Octavian asked. He had stopped the forward momentum of his hips and was standing still. "Did you say something?"

"I did, Master. Did it cause you pain?"

"No, but I'm not sure what it was."

"Me, either." I could feel that whatever it was, it had not worked. Something was wrong, but I was encouraged that at least, something had happened. I wouldn't feel so foolish trying it again. "Let's get back to it, shall we, Master?"

"Absolutely, Servant."

Octavian fell into his rhythm of fucking as easily as a professional soccer player could have bounced a ball on his knee when someone tossed it to him. He was fucking with such determination and power, that I wondered what he was thinking. He blew the smoke from his cigar onto me as he pushed to the depths of my ass.

"As a Romanian marked man, I countermand the curse placed on the Segunda family," I whispered to the grassy floor.

Once again, the wave of sensation started at my head and crashed through my body until it left my feet. Octavian stopped in mid-fuck.

"What the fuck is going on, Jackson?"

"I'm trying something, Master."

"Trying what?"

"To remove the curse, Master," I said, almost sheepishly.

"That is why we are fucking in the ruins of my ancestral estates?"

"Yes, Master. Well, besides the fact that we just like to fuck wherever we are."

He chuckled. "Do you think you can? How do you even know what you are doing?"

"I think that tingling sensation is telling me that I'm getting close, Master."

"Do you think the marked man who cursed us would have been willing to submit to my ancestor?"

I held my breath while I thought about what he was asking. "You mean it might have been against his will, Master?" I had never considered this before.

"Yes. I'm not proud of it, but the Romi have not always been treated with respect."

"Perhaps you should bind my hands behind my back, Master."

"My pleasure, Servant." Octavian grabbed the belt from his jeans and wrapped it around my wrists, binding them to the small of my back. He lowered my face to the grass.

He quickly took up his fucking pace once again. My cock was now painfully hard as my new Master dominated me.

"As a marked man of Romania, I countermand the curse on the Segunda family." This time I said it loudly, even though my mouth was partially crushed against the grassy floor.

This time the tingling sensation started in my shoulders and crashed down my body like the first two.

"Progress, Master. Why don't you throw some of that water on me?"

He doused my back with the sacred water without even breaking his fucking stroke. He put the water bottle down, grabbed my bound hands, and pulled back.

My face rose slightly off the ground. "As a Romanian marked man, I countermand the curse put on the Segunda family."

The tingling started at my waist this time and quickly crashed through me.

"I'm close, Jackson," Octavian said in a hoarse voice. He was fucking my ass like a freaking piston in his sports car.

I only had one more chance. My ass was absolutely on fire and my cock felt like it was going to explode. I needed to do something different.

I whispered, "As my ancestor cursed the Segunda family, I have the power to change that curse." My cum-vent opened as my balls started to churn the cum and send it up the length of my cock.

Octavian's pace was starting to break down. He was on the edge.

I continued, "I change the curse so that the Segunda's can control their invisibility."

Many things happened in the next two seconds — Octavian roared with his release deep inside me, his cock exploded in my guts as he filled me with his hot seed, his weight pushed me off of my knees and flat onto the grass, and my cock pumped hot sticky semen out of me onto my stomach and the grass below me.

I wasn't sure if the tingling sensation had begun in my ass and moved through my legs or whether that was just the sensation of being dominated sexually by my true Master.

I finally came to the conclusion that I had not been able to make the counter-curse in time. There was nothing wrong with trying again later. In fact, I was already looking forward to it.

CHAPTER THIRTY-ONE

The Segunda family tree, as found in the archives of the Bucharest City Library.

July 4, 2019
Spiridon Segunda (1716?-1750)
Decebel Segunda (1738-1762)
Geofri Segunda (1760-1785)
Iancu Segunda (1780-1813) – Nandru Segunda (1778-1785)
Haralamb Segunda (1808-1830) – Costache Segunda (1807-1807) – Benedikte Segunda (1805-1815)
Skender Segunda (1828-1858)
Alexandru (1855-1900) – Atanese Segunda (1852-1853) – Iosif (1851-1851)
Bogdi Segunda (1885-1931)
Omor Segunda (1910-1940) – Ilei Segunda (1907-1919) – Ferka Segunda (1905-1928)
Julis Segunda (1942- present) – Viorel Segunda (1940-1976)
Nicolai Segunda (1959- present)
Octavian Segunda (1980-present)

Octavian and I had just had an amazing fuck session. I had tried to reverse the curse placed on his family, but had come to the conclusion that I had failed and would have to try again another time.

My new Master and I had fallen asleep, exhausted, right there on the soft grassy floor of his ancestral home. His cock had softened and pulled out of me, but his big body kept me warm as he draped over me. He was like a giant hairy comforter that kept me just as comfortable as if I was in a fancy hotel.

I woke up with the sun and desperately needed something to drink. I tried to remember if we had left any drinks in the car, but I thought not. I slid out from under Octavian, who was snoring softly and invisibly beside me.

Well, obviously that did not work . . .

Rolling away from Octavian, I eventually stood up, trying not to wake him. I looked out of the ruined stone windows here in the back of the house and was amazed to see a beautiful blue lake in the near distance surrounded by the forest on all sides except for the one with the house.

I decided to walk down there immediately. There was no reason to get dressed since we were completely alone, so I just put on my shoes and headed out of the ruins of the house.

There was a clear path down to the lake with just a little bit of the forest encroaching upon it. I had an easy time following the trail, but I had to be careful as I negotiated the land quickly dipping down towards the lake.

I was almost to the water when something moved in the bushes ahead of me. I stopped in my tracks as a wolf came out and looked at me. It was soon joined by a second one.

"Shit! Now, I need to be invisible," I said softly to the air.

The wolves suddenly looked confused. They swung their big heads around and looked at each other. I stepped to the side away from them and they did not react.

Am I invisible?

The wolves sniffed the air and whined to each other.

I can't be . . . It's been more than two hours since Octavian and I fucked. His power would be gone now, plus I saw that he was invisible before I left the ruins of the house.

I stepped further to the side and made a noise on the gravel.

The wolves' ears perked up and they turned towards the

sound, but made no move. They made a whining noise and then abruptly turned and headed into the forest.

I stood absolutely still and silent for what felt like hours.

Taking a step towards the water, I carefully watched and listened for the brush to move. Seeing nothing, I headed to the water. I knelt at the edge and dipped my hands into it.

I was so thirsty that I had already drunk two handfuls of water before I noticed that I did not have a reflection on the surface of the lake.

"Son of a bitch!" I said, louder than I would have liked.

"Is this really happening?" I asked in a whisper as I continued to stare at the blank water.

"I want to be visible."

My appearance appeared with such detail and clarity that I fell backwards and landed on my back. I jumped back to my feet and stared at my reflection in the water.

"I fucking did it!" I looked back to the ruins of the house. I wanted to run to Octavian to tell him.

But what if it was just me? Surely I got my power from him, which meant that he had the same ability to control the invisibility.

My backside was covered with dust and leaves, so I decided to get into the lake and get clean before I headed back to the house.

Slowly and carefully, I stepped into the water. It was cold, but felt good on my feet. The bottom was covered in smooth rocks instead of the usual lake silt that I was used to in the United States.

Once I got deep enough to dive under the water, I did, coming up and holding myself against the chill. I watched the land around the lake, expecting to see the wolves again.

I was surprised when I saw the still water ripple near the shore. Instinctively, I stepped back as I saw another ripple. I tripped over a large rock on the bottom and fell backwards into the water.

When I surfaced, hands grabbed me from under the water.

"Don't be frightened, Jackson."

"Master!"

"I saw you in the water and thought it was an excellent idea."

I wasn't sure how to tell him except to blurt it out, but I didn't want that to be the way he found out.

"I have something to show you, Master."

"I've seen your ass before, Jackson," he said dryly.

"No, *this*, Master."

I need to be invisible.

Octavian's hands let go of me as he stepped back from me in the water. I could only tell this by the surface of the water around him. We were both invisible now.

"How is that possible, Jackson?"

I need to be visible.

Octavian's hand slapped at the water.

"Just think it, Master."

"Think it?"

"Say it to yourself."

Suddenly, like a mirage in the desert, my Master appeared before my eyes.

"Excellent, Master."

Octavian looked down at his hands and then back up at me. "You did it?"

"We did it, Master."

"How?"

"I think I might be a descendant of the marked man who originally put the curse on your family. What we did last night allowed me to change it."

"Change it?"

"We can control it now, Master."

He said excitedly as he flashed back and forth between visible and invisible, "Even better than getting rid of the curse,

Jackson."

"I hope it lasts. If it doesn't, we might have to repeat the ceremony from last night, Master."

He smiled and said, "Maybe we have to repeat that every night just to make sure, Servant."

I smiled broadly at him and said, "Absolutely, Master. I can see you now."

"You have always seen me, Jackson."

"And you, me, Master."

ABOUT THE AUTHOR

Crawford Rhine is easily inspired by travelling. His series, The Romanian Chronicles, was inspired by a summer trip to Romania and Russia where he completed four books and has added some since. These books are re-imaginings of the classic movie monsters from the 1930's, updated with new twists like Dracula, Frankenstein, the Werewolf, and the Phantom of the Opera. A recent trip to Switzerland provides the backdrop for the Invisible Man.

Crawford's first series The Master & Servant Series are inspired by sports and occupations that traditionally exude masculinity like baseball, basketball, football, acting, and being a country music star. A trip to Denmark has inspired a book on soccer still to come.

He looks forward to continuing to travel to far-away places and publishing more books in each series.